FORBIDDEN

THE COMPLETE SERIES

JEN KATEMI

Forbidden: The Complete Series
Copyright © 2018 Jen Katemi

ISBN 13: 978-0-6484045-1-4

This Collection includes the previously published titles:
Marriage Games © 2017 Jen Katemi
Alpha Submissive © 2017 Jen Katemi
Watch Me © 2017 Jen Katemi
Breaking the Rules © 2018 Jen Katemi

All Rights Reserved

Published by Flourish Books
Edited by Deadra Krieger
Cover Design by Willsin Rowe

CONTENTS

MARRIAGE GAMES

A SPANKING ROMANCE

PREFACE

On their anniversary weekend away, will a spanking paddle help re-kindle Grace and Henry's waning libido, or will this married couple's first kinky time also be their last?

"When I suggested a weekend away to rekindle the flame of our fifteen-year-old marriage, I had no idea Henry would take it as an opportunity to bust out the credit card at our local sex shop. But now I'm sitting in this country cottage on Saturday night, surrounded by nothing but forest for miles in every direction, and staring at my husband holding the spanking paddle as I wonder if I really have the nerve to bend over and let him use it." ~ *Grace*

CHAPTER 1

GRACE

L ate autumn rain drums hard on the tin roof of the rented holiday cottage, echoing the pounding of my heart as I consider my husband's request.

"Bare that smooth white arse and bend over, Grace. You've been very naughty. You deserve a good spanking."

Not really a request, then. More a demand. An unfamiliar one that resonates between us like something alien has entered the room. Henry looks different, holding up that wooden spanking paddle. His long lean frame, six-foot two-inch height, and tousled black hair have always incited a flutter in my pulse rate. Tonight, those composed blue eyes have a gleam of hard polished ice in them, and his mouth—normally curved up in an easy grin—is set firm like he really means business. Even his voice sounds altered. As always, the melodic tones are deep and undoubtedly familiar, but there's an unusually authoritative edge that says, "Do as I say or else." The demand accelerates the ripple of excitement scudding through my veins.

This enigmatic stranger is a damn sight sexier than the

predictable partner I was expecting when I booked our anniversary weekend away.

We arrived only a couple of hours ago in the grey gloom of early evening. The secluded cottage set in these quiet forest surrounds ignited an immediate squiggle of anticipation deep inside. I could scream my heart out in the orgasm of the century here, and no one would be around to hear it except my husband.

I've always known about the hint of darkness that lurks within him—that longing to push the boundaries in our sexual relationship. It should be easy, given my own secret needs, to indulge in a bit of kinky play now and then. We complement each other—we always have. Yet, during our fifteen years together, there's always been a reluctance to acknowledge what we see in the depths of each other's eyes. What if one of us takes it too far? It happened to me, once, before I met Henry, and it nearly killed me.

Since then, I've tamped down everything not vanilla into a hidden little compartment deep inside my mind, and I think Henry must have taken his cue from me and done the same. My husband is composed, logical, and carefully considered in his approach to life. *Always*. I am, too. We're the embodiment of calm, according to our family and friends, and that's no mean feat when everything inside—at least for me—is screaming to get out and silently railing at the bland ordinariness of our life together.

Back when we met, about a year after my first marriage ended, Henry had a wild, dangerous edge that immediately attracted and held my attention, even as it scared me silly to think I might be heading straight back into chaos once again. I was still recovering from what happened the previous year, but he was so fascinating, with that mysterious combination of uncompromising power and gentle amusement, that it was impossible to stay away. I haven't seen that hard edge in years, and I hardly recognize the man standing before me. My masochistic side yearns to respond to the gleam of authority revealed in that slightly twisted grin.

Couples counseling. Who knew, when we started attending sessions a few months ago, that we'd end up here in this country cottage, surrounded by forest for miles in every direction, and with permission from our therapist to indulge our every deviant fantasy?

"Be true to yourselves," the counselor said at our last session. "If you don't, then you're not being fair to each other, or to your marriage."

She's right. We've been hiding behind a façade of normality, or rather, I forced us *both* into ignoring our hidden needs, and now our marriage is wobbling under the continued strain of trying to be something we're not.

This weekend *has* to work, because the alternative is unthinkable. My parents divorced when I was ten—the same age our twins are now. I can't imagine ever putting our children through the trauma my siblings and I went through. And yet, I'm so wound up I don't know *how* to be me anymore. It's as if Henry and I have stifled our natural inclinations for so long we've lost the essence of *us*.

In a way it feels like tonight is our very first time, and my cheeks are hot with the flush of expectation and anxiety.

"*Now*, Grace. I'm waiting." Impatience flares briefly in his features, and then disappears behind the stranger's mask. This is my husband and yet somehow, it's not.

My instinct is to immediately bend down and grab my ankles; let him do whatever he wants. The wet slickness that coats the seam between my legs is testament to how much I want to comply. My mind has yet to catch up with my body,

7

though, and for some reason it won't release the fear that is still holding me captive.

So I play for time and challenge him instead. "Why are you talking like that?" I know why. Of course I do, and yet these stupid questions spill out of my mouth. "Since when is *that* your thing?" I nod toward the paddle he's cradling. It's a style I would have bought myself, if I'd had the nerve. It's quite large—a good beginner tool, because the larger head diffuses the impact. It's made of wood, and I can see one side is cushioned with a padded leather cover. Henry is stroking that side on his palm. Clearly he loves the feel of it against his skin, and I have to confess, the thought of that leather caressing my body sends a signal straight to my sex. A breath catches in my throat as my long-dormant clit awakes with a throb.

This weekend might be just what we need, after all.

A slap echoes through the room in a loud staccato and I jump, but he's struck his own palm, not me. I catch a sudden glitter in his eyes before it's gone, equally fast. That glimpse shows me just how much Henry really wants this, and I shiver at the realization that I'm going to get a proper spanking tonight.

He smacks the paddle against his palm a second time, and then starts to circle around me, pacing slowly as if studying my form. He pauses when he reaches my back, and a caress meanders down my spine. It's too rigid to be his fingers. It feels firm and yet somehow slightly squishy. Perhaps he has the paddle on its edge, angled more toward the padded leather side? Goose bumps form along the wandering trail he creates, and when he reaches my butt cheeks he keeps going, sliding the implement into my crevice and continuing the forward swipe.

I look down and see the edge poking out from my mound,

and then it swivels slightly until the flat side rests against my pussy.

"Time to do what you're told, Gracie." His voice sounds much closer than I expect. A puff of breath warms my skin in that sensitive crick between shoulder and neck, and I arch my head almost involuntarily to one side, willing him to kiss me there. He doesn't, but his mouth is so close my nerve endings react as if he has. Somehow, he has branded me without a single touch of his lips.

"Have you...um..." I swallow and try again. "Have you always wanted to do this? Spank me?" A ripple of titillation rolls across my skin.

He taps me, just a light pat against my pussy, and I bite my lip to contain the whimper. *What will it feel like, when he gives me a proper spanking? Against my arse, if I'm a good girl and do as he wishes. How hard will he go? How much will it hurt? Will my butt turn pink under his hand?* The random thoughts send the growing heat between my legs into overdrive and my channel clenches in a sudden, unexpected reflex. I arch my back a little, trying to give him better access, but the paddle disappears as he reverses it back along my seam and out the way it came.

Henry continues his circling study of my body and ends up in front of me again. He's already buck-naked and his erection is enormous—full and hard and the tip all shiny with pre-cum. I can smell sex on him. The scent of desire. It mixes with his own masculine flavor in an alluring blend of light citrus and heavier musky spice that I've loved since the first moment I met him. A corresponding wave of desire sends another stronger shiver traversing my skin.

My nipples begin to ache as if someone has scraped across their surface with a fingernail, and they pebble into hardness. It's as if my body is coming alive after a long period of inertia. His gaze shifts until he's staring right at my erect nipples. I'm wearing a see-through, short red negligee that I bought online a couple of weeks ago, and the hem just skims the top of my thighs while triangular cut out sections in the top allow my breasts to poke hungrily out toward him.

I showered and put on the lingerie as soon as we arrived, and immediately felt sexier than I have in years. I knew it would turn him on. He loves my breasts, *and* my ass. In this outfit he gets easy access to both.

There's a sudden craving in Henry's features that I haven't seen in so long, and the throbbing in my clit ramps up a couple of notches. My pussy is heavy and aching, my vaginal lips swollen, and it's becoming difficult to keep my legs together. All I can think of is what it would be like to have my husband's face right there at that juncture between my thighs. Tasting. Licking. Sucking. Teasing my engorged clit out of its hiding place and right into his mouth as he forces me into submission with his tongue.

Oh, God, I want him to taste me so much. Or fuck me. Or both. Only… My eyes shift to the paddle he's now slapping lightly against his thigh. He wants to *spank* me first.

Another quiver shakes my frame and his eyes meet mine. They're unreadable, icy, and calm. "You still don't want to play, then?" I can't tell whether he is disappointed, or starting to become angered at the idea that I might not ever be open to this.

Slowly I shake my head. "I didn't say that." *Look between my legs. Can't you see my clit? Can't you tell how swollen it is, how wet I am, just imagining you dishing out that punishment?*

"It's our anniversary, Gracie. How long since we really had fun in the bedroom?"

"I…" My mouth opens and closes a couple of times as I

try to recall. "I can't remember." Since the twins came along, any kind of romance has well and truly fallen by the wayside. Sex has become something to be endured as a duty. Fun? Nope, not part of the equation.

Especially so this past year, when our son's tantrums and behavior issues seemed to escalate and we were finally given the diagnosis we always knew in our hearts. On the autism spectrum. Such a relief to *know* at last, and to officially begin the process of learning how to manage it for all of us.

The effect on Henry and I has been...*difficult*, to say the least, particularly in the sense of maintaining any kind of intimacy in our marriage. Add to that the tamping down of our natural desires, and we might as well be brother and sister, for all the *fun* we've had in recent years.

That's one of the reasons I rented this secluded cottage practically in the middle of nowhere and organized my sister to look after the kids for the weekend. In the hope that we could begin to rediscover whatever it is we need to do to save our waning relationship.

"I don't know. It's not really what I—"

The unreadable mask drops and his face is so crestfallen my words choke to a stop. Why am I so afraid? What is it about letting go in front of him that has me tied up in knots? I've *fantasized* about this, for God's sake. I buy erotic books and read them avidly, trying to relive everything that's missing in our relationship. I've started looking things up on the internet, too, when I'm home on my own during the day. Remembering what it feels like to have those twin sensations of pleasure and pain play out across my body. The intensity of pain and the exquisite release of pleasure that follows. One without the other has never been quite enough, and yet I've had to make it so with Henry. Until now.

What if it ends up happening again? What if... I wrestle

11

that thought to a stop. Henry is not like the other one. And we have to try this. We *have* to.

He's standing by the open fire, coated in shades of flickering golden light. There's no shyness between us, not anymore, but as soon as he pulled that paddle out of his overnight bag and held it up, something shifted inside me. Coyness exploded in my gut. The strange mix of trepidation and excitement is still making itself felt even several minutes later, causing my heart to pound almost too hard against the wall of my chest.

Go with it. For once, just go with it and stop overanalyzing everything. Trust him to control how far this goes. Let yourself submit. The thoughts tumble around my brain like leaves in the wind.

I take a deep breath and hold it in an attempt to steady my nerves, and then I let it out slow with a deliberate smile aimed at my husband. *I* can *do this*. "Okay then, Henry. What else have you got tucked away in that little bag of tricks?"

His quick grin lights up the room and takes ten years off his face. "Oh, I've got lots of fun things in my bag. Though you're not going to sample any of them unless you're a good girl and do exactly as I say."

My heart skips a beat before resuming its patter doubly fast. Play time. "Well, I *have* been a naughty girl, Sir. So naughty. What are you going to do about it?"

CHAPTER 2

HENRY

When Gracie gives me that sultry, challenging look I almost shoot my load then and there. And it's a bloody huge load I'm carrying right about now. Last time we had sex was... *yeah*. Can't exactly remember. A couple of months ago, maybe? Last time I jacked off alone was a super-quick effort in the shower about three weeks ago. In our house you never get much "alone" time.

Blue balls? Mine are practically purple.

I was so wired on the drive here I thought I was going to crash twice on that narrow, winding country road. What if I ask her to do something that makes her feel bad about us? About *me*? What if she takes one look at all the toys I bought at the sex shop and jumps back in the car to drive straight home again? I'm staking everything on that one comment she made a couple of weeks ago. The night we were watching some show on TV where this woman went back in time and married a Scottish guy. Grace looked right at me while the guy was giving his wife an erotic spanking, and said, "Do you ever wonder what it'd be like to have the time and space to act out some of the sexual fantasies we keep in *here*?" She tapped a long finger against her temple, and then right afterward she went and booked this cottage.

Spanking? She wants to be spanked? I've fantasized about doing that to my wife practically since the day I met her. I know a few details about what happened to her before, and it nearly tore her apart. That bastard ex of hers kept her tied up alone in the hotel room for so long that she ended up in the hospital. She has permanent nerve damage in her left wrist, and a slight limp too. One of her ankles never quite recovered.

I purposely stayed away from the cuffs and any kind of restraints in my little shopping spree. She's so scared of what might happen that she's all buttoned up these days. I *get* it. I do. I won't ever put her through anything like that again. But I have needs. Needs that are becoming far more urgent, and if I can't indulge soon I don't know what's going to happen.

I *love* Grace. She and the kids are my *everything*, and yet there's a part of me deep down that's being eaten up by this blackness that needs to get out. I'm not a sadist, as such, but I need to be in control. I need to take charge and *dominate*, for fuck's sake. And I want to push my submissive wife's boundaries until she has no choice except to completely submit to my whim.

Maybe she's finally ready. The counseling helps, I think, because a lot of what Grace went through before we got together has finally come to light. Things even *I* didn't know. Jeez, I'd like to fucking *kill* that prick. He nearly destroyed this beautiful woman, and all because she screamed too loud and embarrassed him. So he left her there, and never went back.

He has no fucking idea what it's really like to top someone. Yes, you dominate, but you also *care*. You don't abuse. It's not rocket science.

After the night Grace booked this place, I couldn't *stop* thinking about making my fantasy a reality. I love her rounded butt. It's a lot plumper these days than it was when we were first going out, and that makes it even more to my taste. The thought of turning all that prized white flesh a delicate pink under my hand, or even better, with this paddle, has had me halfway hard ever since.

Yeah. This weekend couldn't come fast enough.

When we stepped onto the wrap-around veranda and walked in to the cottage and I saw that fire already burning brightly in the grate, all I could think about was my wife bent over in front of it holding her ankles or calves in a classic position of submission. The firelight would turn her creamy skin a warm golden orange, and her bum would develop a bright pink tinge as I brand her with my mark.

And now here we are, and she looks even more amazing than I imagined, standing here beside the fire. Sexier than I've ever seen her, actually. Her curves are definitely golden and warm in the light, with flickering shadows adding depth and complexity to the view. Shades of darkness that didn't exist in my imagination. Her brown, shoulder-length hair is usually scraped back in a messy ponytail, but tonight she's wearing it down. It's full of waves and appears extra-shiny in the firelight. Her hazel eyes have softened from their habitual sharp intelligence to a more accessible greenish brown, and she looks mysterious as well as sexy in that see-through red nightie.

Her breasts are full, though they do sit lower than they used to before the kids. Those cut-out bits in her top allow the curved flesh to thrust outward and show off the pointy pink tips. Her nipples and the area around them have always been enticingly large and tonight, even more than usual, they are crying out to be sucked. I have a couple of clamps in my toy bag that could perfectly adorn those nipples later on. First though, I intend to put this naughty little minx over my knee.

She wants it too. There's something in her eyes, a wildness maybe, which I've only ever seen once or twice before. That night a few years ago when we both had too much to drink and our base desires started to crawl toward the surface... I *loved* that night. I use it to fuel my fantasies whenever I'm on my own. I know she sees it differently, though. Ever since then she's even more buttoned up, cutting herself off from any kind of intimacy whatsoever. Shame? Maybe a little. Worry I'll lose it like that fucking cocksucker ex-husband of hers? Yeah, no doubt. I *won't*. Though if she hasn't learnt to trust me by now, after all this time... *Fuck*, we need this. For her sake. And for ours.

Tonight my wife's eyes promise wild and wicked, and my shaft jerks in recognition of what she's really like, deep down inside. *Yeah. That's her. That's the one I want. Let her out, Gracie.*

"Well, Sir? What are you going to do about it?" When she throws out that challenge for the second time her voice is husky. *Naughty girl.* My dick aches so bad—especially when she adds in the honorific *Sir* in such a provocative tone—it's almost impossible not to take it in hand and stroke. When I was young my erections were almost vertical, but these days they're usually a bit more toward half-mast. Tonight, when I glance down, the hungry eye of my cock looks straight back up at me, glistening with a drop of pre-cum, and I can't help the burst of pride that lifts my lips. The old man can still get it up. Right up, it seems.

Grace turns and sashays across the rug, her limp barely noticeable in the subdued light from the fire. She heads toward that comfortable-looking old couch, and I study her rounded ass, considering where I'm going to lay the first stroke. Left cheek? Or right? Either choice will be equally as good as the other. Her behind offers two perfect globes of flesh, their creamy expanse crying out for my disciplinary touch. I look down at the paddle in my hand, and instinct tells me to start this the old-fashioned way. With my hand. We can graduate to the paddle later.

I lay the implement on the side table next to the couch, then step around her to sit down and make myself as comfortable as I can. It's hard to appear relaxed when so much adrenalin is pumping through my system that my hands are literally shaking. Grace looks nervous too, and it's up to me to take the lead. I pat my thigh encouragingly. "What am I going to do about it? Naughty girls need a decent spanking to teach them how to behave. Come here, over my knee. You know this'll be for your own good, and you know what? You're just gonna have to suck it up and take it, baby."

My voice is rough and when she glances down at me there's a blush turning her cheeks a delicate pink. Her mouth purses momentarily into a perfect little "oh" and I imagine those sexy lips wrapped around me. Hot, moist, and tight. My dick jerks so hard it hurts.

Play the game.

"Over my knee. *Now.*" I inject authority into my tone and raise an eyebrow, trying for calm and wondering if she can detect my racing pulse. Is it visible at the base of my neck? I can feel it there, pounding as if I've just done a sprint.

I've been waiting for this moment so long that now it's here I feel awkward. Like a novice once again, which I suppose I am really, after all this time. Novice or not, though, my cock is full and hard, and my fingers itch to tan her rear and assert my authority. I won't do that, ever, until she agrees to play too. I point to my lap, determined to ensure my wife will do as she's told.

Grace

If it was anyone else who spoke to me that way I'd tell them to eff off, but this is *Henry*, and he looks hotter than I can ever remember. More macho and confident than usual. His background is what we always joke about as hybrid, being a mix of Australian, English, and Italian, and that heritage has given him a gorgeous olive complexion and smooth skin that looks as if he has a permanent date with a tanning salon. Sitting there on the couch, with one of his arms resting casually along the back and the other pointing commandingly to his lap, he's tanned, fit, and seems far younger than his forty-two years. I swallow down my defensive words and give him a tentative smile instead.

He wants me over his knee? "Yes, Sir! But…"

There's one thing I have to confirm first, and when one of his eyebrows begins to rise I add quickly, "Safe word, Sir. What should—"

"*Red*. You need to slow it down, say yellow. You need to stop? Use red." His tone is decisive and clipped.

"Okay. Yellow, or red."

I climb onto the couch and kneel beside him, hesitating for a moment. I'm tempted to lean down and take his erect shaft into my mouth. I can see veins winding around that hard flesh, their distended form testament to the amount of blood that is holding the organ rigid. The tip, shaped like a neat little helmet, is shiny with pre-cum fluid. It's been so long I can hardly recall what he tastes like, and I remember I used to love it. A caress on the curve of my butt distracts me from my memories of fellatio, and then a light slap reminds me that he really means business.

"Sorry, Sir." I bend further across his lap, stifling a quick giggle. Tonight is probably the first time I've ever called him *Sir*. "Don't get too used to this!" I mutter that last bit into the arm of the couch, where my face has ended up, but another slap, more firm this time and delivered across my rear, tells me he heard what I said.

"That's disrespectful. I could get *very* used to this."

The warm tingling in my pussy tells me *I* could, too. I know from past experience that spanking can stimulate the circulation in your genitals, enhancing the erotic pleasure, and from the increasingly heavy ache between my legs I can't even imagine what it'll be like when he really starts in on my butt.

Even though this position feels awkward at first, with his erection huge and hard and hot against my side, I'm hyper-aware of the throbbing in my clit as I rest my pussy against his muscled thigh. I wriggle a little, both an attempt to get more comfortable and because the compulsion to ease that ache by thrusting my hips becomes almost overwhelming. I press my closed mouth right into the arm of the couch in an attempt to hold in a groan.

My fidgeting has an added benefit. Henry's cock shifts between us and I'm rewarded with a sharp intake of his breath from above, and then a slow release of air between his teeth. I can't see his face from this position bent over his knee, but I know him so well I can imagine his blue eyes half-closed and desire pulling his generous lips taut. I love knowing how hard it is for him to hold on. I *want* him on the edge. It adds to my own pleasure.

I wriggle again, deliberately thrusting back and forth against him. The movement creates a strange contradiction of firm and soft as my mound smacks into the hard muscle of his leg and then releases. In between thrusts the light springy hair on his thigh tickles my clit with such delicacy that eventually I can't hold in that recalcitrant groan. It forces its way up and out of my throat, and I clutch at the couch in reflexive action.

He grunts. "Stay still, babe. No more movement until *I* say you can." The tone is imposing. It doesn't sound like him, and because I have my back to him it's almost as if I'm displaying my privates to a complete stranger. My wet and greedy pussy, opening up like a damp pink flower right there in front of his eyes.

A slow blush heats my face, rolling uncomfortably upward from my neck in a blanket of warmth, until his comforting and familiar masculine scent rises around me. The wave of shyness recedes and I lean more firmly into his shaft, sandwiching the hard flesh between our bodies and continuing to grind my mound against his leg.

Fingertips gently graze my skin as he lifts the negligee up and out of the way. Goose bumps form where he touches and I let out a satisfied sigh. It feels good. Familiar. I relax on his lap, closing my eyes and sinking in to the moment. The pop and crackle of the fire is a soothing background noise punctuated only by the sound of rain peppering the roof. Today has been a precursor to winter, with its cold winds and incessant rain. It's a perfect night to nestle in front of an open fire and cocoon ourselves away from the real world outside. And then after, there's a huge spa in the bathroom, and an electric blanket on the big four-poster bed with its light puffy duvet just waiting for us to slide beneath it to cuddle.

His breathing has grown so harsh I know my wriggling has increased the arousal for him as much as me, and my grin is wide as my face presses into the fabric.

The firm smack on my bottom comes out of nowhere and I lift my head, yelping at the sudden sting. "*Ow*! Henry!" It's more surprise than pain, though. I wasn't quite ready. Just as I begin to relax he does it again, and then again, each stroke becoming stronger as if he's testing out how far he can go with his punishment.

Each time he does it my whole body jerks in reaction. I try to stay still, but it's hard when there's a burning pain being delivered across your rear and you can't anticipate when the stroke will arrive. I grit my teeth, trying to pre-judge his actions, even though he's not consistent with the blows. To make things more difficult, Henry's other hand is sandwiched deep between my legs, exploring fingers caressing my inner thighs and brushing against my swollen labia lips with a tenderness that belies the spanking message.

Punishment. And pleasure. The twin sensations send conflicting signals to my brain. "You're messing with my head, love." I manage to gasp the words after one particularly hard smack, which he follows with a light dance of fingertips deep into my seam. I'm damp with sweat and desire, and it's an easy glide for him up and down my slit.

"Good. I *want* you messed up, Grace. I want you so messed up you don't care what we do to each other. I want you to forget convention, and I want you to *remember…*" One of his fingers reaches up into my vaginal channel, and another is toying with my anus. He's never touched me in the latter spot before, and it feels so damn good.

"Remember what?" My voice is throaty and I can hardly get the words out.

"Remember who you really are."

CHAPTER 3

GRACE

Another light smack, and then he flicks my asshole. A moan escapes between my clenched teeth. "Do you like this?"

"No." A shudder runs through me, contradicting my denial.

"Liar." He spanks me again, and the smarting discomfort generates tears in the corners of my eyes. "Don't lie. I won't have it. It's wicked."

Desire follows the pain. I don't *want* to enjoy this. I don't want *him* to enjoy this. But I do, and he does, and we know each other too damn well. "Sorry, Sir."

"Let's try it again." I bite my bottom lip as he flicks back and forth over my anus. "Do you like this?"

The sensation is extraordinary, ramping up the desire tenfold. His other finger is still deep inside my channel, filling my emptiness with his touch. *It's okay. This is Henry. Just tell him the truth.* "Yes. I do." My breath hisses out noisily with the reluctant admission.

"Good. How about *this*?" Before I understand what he's

about to do, he breaches my anus with the tip of his finger. I'm so wet it doesn't really hurt, and I don't think he's gone in more than a centimeter or two. It feels full, and weird, and so fucking *good* that I want to buck against his hand until I come.

"Yes, oh yes." My groan turns almost to a sob and I give in to the temptation. I have to move. I *have* to. I push up against his hand, urging him deeper. "I *love* that. I want more."

I feel him shift close. His breath is coming quickly, in and out, puffing against my hair and heating my ear. When he speaks his tone is low and urgent, and I can hear the excitement lying beneath. "Now you're being *really* naughty. I told you not to move unless I gave permission."

This time it's a barrage of punishing smacks on my rear, and it burns like hell. Even as the scalding pain explodes across my butt cheeks I feel his fingers moving deeper inside me. Exploring my twin channels. Searching out the sweet spots, and eventually finding the jackpot. I want to groan and scream and cry, all at the same time.

Panting. I can hear it, and it's coming from me. "*Henry.*" I gasp, not even sure what I'm asking. "Oh *fuck*, Henry. I can't hold on much longer. I *can't…*"

The climax is building. I can feel it, and I can't stop it, and I can't speak any longer to let him know. He's already aware. How can he not be, with my channels clenching so tightly around his fingers, and my breath coming so uncontrolled, and my whole body hunching with the tension as I ride the inexorable wave toward orgasm? I'm heading fast to that place where thought ends and pure physical sensation takes over. His fingers penetrate even deeper as he slams his hand back and forth between my clenching cheeks and his furious strokes on my ass echo the frenzy within.

Faster, almost frantic now, his finger fuck keeps pace with the spanking. The wave builds until I can't hold it in any longer and I let the orgasm wash over me with a reluctant scream that rips at my throat.

Sensation. Desire. Need. Pain. Guilt.

Tears are dripping from my eyes at the smarting pain even as my muscles clench hard around his fingers. My body, at least, doesn't want to let go even that small physical part of him. I rock back and forth across his lap, crying now for real as I can't even remember the last time I experienced anything so physically overwhelming. I want to let go, completely, with my mind as well as my body, but...

"I screamed, Henry. I screamed. I'm so sorry. So—"

"Shh." My punishment is finally over and he is stroking me instead, the same hand he used to spank me now caressing my back and the curve of my rear with gentle care. *He's not angry.* "It's okay, darling. I've got you. I've got you, Grace."

It's not like my first marriage. It's not. I screamed too loud last time and he got annoyed and left me. After I figured out he wasn't ever coming back, I broke my ankle trying to get out of the restraints. Henry would never do that to me. *Never...*

"I *love* the sound of your screams, baby. I've *missed* them. So much."

I twist my upper body so I can look up into his eyes and when I see the truth of his love, I can finally relax. *Safe.*

Escape into oblivion. Finally, I can fully let go. Finally, I'm there.

He continues to whisper sweet words of comfort in my ear, although I'm too zoned out to concentrate properly on what he's saying. Eventually though, the soothing sound of his voice brings me back, and I realize he's kissing me gently on the back of my neck. I *love* being kissed there. He knows it, too, and he does it again, and then again, as if to make up for the fury of the spanking he administered only a few short minutes ago.

"That did hurt."

The hand stroking my back stills, and then he grips my shoulder and helps me to sit up. There are tissues on the side table, thank God, and he reaches over to snag a couple and hand them to me. I'm an ugly crier, unfortunately, and when I do cry my nose runs as freely as my tears. "You didn't like the spanking, then?"

Laughter tries to bubble up out of my chest but I hold it in. Instead, I wipe my nose and manage a trembly grin. "No. I hated it. Couldn't you tell?"

His frown is instant and he looks down at his hands as if they are foreign objects he's never seen before. He clenches them, tight, and I wonder if his nails are digging into his palms. The knuckles are white. "I'm so sorry, hon, I thought—"

"I'm joking, love. For God's sake, Henry! Coming like that...my orgasm was so strong it nearly tore me in two. Couldn't you tell from the scream?" I repeat my previous phrase for good measure. "I *loved* it!"

"Oh." He unclenches his fists and I see he has created little crescent marks on his palms. "I...I guess I hoped, but—"

I laugh again, only this time I don't bother trying to hold it in. I think maybe he needs to hear it. I reach out and capture one of his hands in my own, stroking my thumb across his injured palm. His lips remain tight for a moment longer, and then the tautness leaves his face as he joins in chuckling.

My heart skips a beat. How long has it been since I heard him laugh? Once again my husband sounds like a stranger.

"Oh *God*, Henry! What happened to us? When did things get so…sad?"

"Don't know, love." There's a jerkiness to the shrug that accompanies his words, and then it hits me. I've forgotten all about his needs. His erection is massive, and leaking so much juice from the tip that his whole organ is glistening. I'm sitting here, happily coming back down to Earth in my own sweet time, and he must be in agony, waiting patiently to fulfil his own desire.

He glances at the paddle and I suck in a breath and hold it. When he used his hand it was manageable, but the paddle? That might push me… What if I can't stop once we start? What if *he* can't? What if one or both of us go too far down *that* road?

There's a hidden part of me that is always afraid of what my husband might think if I really let him see how much I want this. Pain. I crave it. Not always, and not too much. Just enough that when I did let go in the past, the need bubbled up and out of me without any brakes whatsoever. It destroyed my first marriage…

It'll be different tonight. Here in the forest, miles away from any other person, it's just the two of us, safe in our little nest where I can finally let down my guard. And this is *Henry*. He's nothing like the other one. Nothing at all.

I look up and see the impatience in his eyes, and yet I also see the softness of love. *It'll be okay.* He nods as if he knows exactly what I'm thinking, and my heart swells as I realize just how lucky I am to have this man in my life. "Let go." His tone is encouraging, and at the same time I can tell he won't put up with any more nonsense. "From now on I'm in charge. You'll do what I say, and I promise I will look after you. I won't allow it to go too far."

He wraps strong fingers around one of my wrists and lifts

it up between us. It's my left wrist. The one that sustained most of the damage last time. Some of the skin surface is still numb, but not all of it. His thumb moves back and forth, caressing me. Grounding me. "I won't restrain you," he says softly. "We'll leave that as a maybe for the future. Tonight though, I'm warning you. I *will* need more than a simple butt spanking."

He won't restrain me? I pull experimentally against his grip and he immediately lets go of my wrist, true to his word.

A shiver, equal parts fear and anticipation, vibrates through me. I *know* what's inside of him. I've always known, I think. There's a darkness in Henry that's kept tightly on a leash. He would never hurt me, not really. Not unless I ask for it.

And I never have, because I'm just as tightly controlled as he is, and I can't afford to let my inner cravings out. The whole family relies on me to keep the peace. To manage the anger and the tantrums that have been a feature of our lives since the twins were born and Aiden's behavior issues first began to manifest. If I let go that control, even for a day, won't chaos take hold instead?

It's tearing me apart, the never letting go, and in that impatient hunger seated in Henry's eyes I see, perhaps for the first time, how much it is tearing him apart, too. In the end, if we can't be true to ourselves, then we're not being true to our relationship. And I *do* trust him. I do.

"Okay." I nod because he's right. Time to let out this hidden beast that lurks deep inside the both of us.

I release my breath in a rush and reach out to run a finger through the clear liquid seeping from his cock. My hands are shaking so much I have trouble connecting at first, but when I finally do, I bring the nectar to my lips for a taste. His eyes follow the movement with a ravenous look. I suck on my digit, smiling around it, then pop it free.

"Henry." My voice wobbles, and I close my eyes for a second, before opening them again and meeting his gaze squarely. "Isn't it time to show off some of your toys?"

CHAPTER 4

HENRY

I lunge for the paddle and clasp it before she can change her mind. She wants me to paddle her? Now it's *me* who hesitates, just for a moment, as I gauge whether I'm still in control. Can I do this? Bring real pain and pleasure to the woman I love, when I know how afraid she is to walk that delicate tightrope?

My cock is weeping and my chest is heaving as if I'm in the midst of a marathon. "Get up. I need—" What the hell *do* I need? *More*, that's for damn sure. My breath has caught and held in my throat as she obediently gets up off the couch and stands in front of me. She lifts her arms and slides the red nightie up and over her head, giving it a light toss away from the open fire. It puddles on the floor several feet away, in a pile of shapeless red. My wife now stands fully naked before me, her creamy skin glowing in the firelight, her brown hair all tousled and wild looking, and her pussy is directly in line with my gaze.

After fifteen years it should be a familiar sight, and yet there's something about Grace tonight that I just can't put my finger on. She's sexier than I've ever seen her. *So fucking sexy*. I feel like a teenager again, with excited butterflies causing strange pangs in my stomach.

This is what it felt like, that first time we made love. Not the fooling around beforehand, but *that* moment. You know the one, when there's a sudden realization that it's actually going to happen. For real. For the very first time.

My heart is pounding and I reach out to stroke her clit, just lightly, where I can see it poking out from her slit. The heat warms my fingertips, even with that lightest of touches. She hisses out a breath and her eyes half close as she gazes down at me. She's trembling. I can feel it beneath my hand. I can see the wobble in her stance.

"Do you really want this, Grace? If you want me to stop, just say so. Any time."

Her laughter is brief and her eyes flash with some kind of emotion that I can't quite read. "Do you hear me using our safe word?"

That cheekily arched brow that accompanies her words sends a thrill through my whole system. My stomach clenches again as the butterflies go nuts. I don't think I was this nervous the first time we had sex. It was the third date, and we were still so young, and even then I knew she was going to be someone special in my life. I wanted the first time to be perfect for both of us. Just like tonight.

"Can't hear anything, my love. You'll need to say it louder."

She puffs out a breath, slow and shaky. "Please. Don't stop. I…want this."

"Good girl."

I point with the paddle to the floor, and this time she moves immediately. Down in front of the fireplace, resting on her hands and knees on the thick pile rug laid out in front of the hearth. Her head bows submissively, and my instinct is to ram my raging boner home, hard and fast. First, I'm going to give her what we both need. I kneel behind her, glad of the rug that cushions me, and study my wife's voluptuous rear. *There*. I pinpoint the exact place I'll start, and after a moment's hesitation I swing the paddle down.

Smack! The sound vibrates through the air just as thoroughly as my stroke vibrates her ass cheek. She gasps, and then lets out another strangled sound as I strike again.

"That's far more intense than when you used your hand." Her admission is breathless and clipped.

God, I want to fuck her so bad. "Punishment is never meant to be easy. You'll know next time to be a good girl. Won't you?"

"Yes. Yes, Sir."

I'm right-handed, and it's her right cheek taking most of the punishment. The flesh pinks up quickly, so I swap to her other side to even it out. As the spanking continues, her gasps become moans. She turns her head, clearly trying to glance over her shoulder toward her rear, and I grab a handful of her hair to stop the movement. "Stay where you are."

I need her to know I'm in charge right now, but it's so difficult to stay focused when all I want to do is bury my shaft to the hilt in her gorgeous body. I'm losing the rhythm. I can't concentrate. And her whimpers are starting to sound like some kind of caged animal.

"Oh, *Henry*." There's so much emotion in her voice, I can't tell if she's enjoying this. Is she making those sounds out of pleasure or pain? Or both?

Her ass is bright pink and her pelvis is thrusting up and down as if dry-humping the air. The slick wetness coating her seam calls to me, and I'm tempted to lift her up so I can sink my face right there into the damp heat between her legs. Instead I run my hand over the rounded curve of her buttocks, enjoying the smoothness of her skin and warming my palm with the heat she's holding there. I knead her flesh a little, trying to spread some of that heat outward from the concentrated red patch.

Time to change tack, before I cream the both of us way too early. I leave her for a moment and retrieve my bag, thinking carefully about what I can use that won't send Grace straight back into her brittle protective shell.

She clearly enjoys an element of pain, but I will not use restraints. I tap my chin, considering, watching her there on hands and knees as her hips continue to buck a little. The movement sets her breasts swinging gently from side to side, and inspiration strikes. She has gorgeous breasts, full and fleshy with large dark-pink nipples that I love to suckle. I reach in to my bag and pull out a pair of nipple clamps I've been imagining on her ever since I bought them.

They're butterfly-style with an adjustable tension, better for beginners than clothes-peg, as I wasn't sure about her pain threshold. A silver chain connects the two clips, and I can't wait to get these into place. She glances up as I touch her shoulder and her eyes widen when she sees what I'm holding, and then she nods.

I gesture, giving her permission to get up off all fours. Before I place the clamps though, I bend right down and do what I've been longing to do this whole time and take one of her already erect nipples into my mouth. I suck hard, moistening and stretching the pebbled tip until she moans above me, and then I do the same to her other side. She tastes fresh and clean, and her light floral perfume rises around me. She is everything I've ever wanted in a woman, and I love her so much.

When I raise my head, her lips are parted and her eyes are shimmering, more green than brown, and I'm struck by how often her eyes change to match her mood. I grab a tissue and dry off her nipples, then quickly attach the clamps in place, taking joy in her grunt and shudder as I do so. A spurt of liquid shoots from my cock in response. I know how much those things hurt. I tried them on myself just to see what it felt like. Not something *I* enjoy, though I can smell the heady musk of sex suddenly wafting up from my wife, mingling with her delicate perfume, and I have to admit to a faint sense of relief. *Thank God. She's not repelled by these clips.*

I have to move fast now, or I'm going to come all over the floor. I lift the silver chain and place it in her mouth, across her moist tongue, loving the shocked look in her eyes as she stares up at me. I use the edge of the paddle to urge her down again onto all fours. "That puts you in charge of your own pain levels, babe. At least for your breasts. You lift your head and it will pull your nipples outward. Tuck your chin into your chest if it's too much. Drop the chain altogether and use your safe word the moment you want them off."

She nods and then groans loudly at the resultant pull. Her whole body trembles. *Jesus, she's sexy.*

I'm more than ready, and I kneel behind her, the head of my dick poking into her seam. I raise the paddle and use it to trace her hip and a whimper escapes her lips. A whimper that sounds so pure, so full of unspoken desire, that I almost cream her rear prematurely.

It's painful to hold on, but I'm determined to wait until she's ready once more. Next time, we will both come together.

I put my arm around her hip and find her clit with the edge of the paddle. Sliding it up along her slit and back again incites a gasp from her, and I flick my wrist to give her a light tap on her pussy lips. She jerks beneath me. I do it again, enjoying the uneven puffs of breath she tries so hard to contain.

I know those clamps are ramping up her pain level when she moves, and I don't want to take her too far, too fast. This is, essentially, our first real play time together, and I have no idea how far I can take her.

"Grace, I want to spank you there, right across your clit..." Would that punishment be too much for her? Would there be only pain? Or would the mixture of pleasure and pain heat her clit so much that the extra blood creates a more intense orgasm? If I give her a slap or two right...*there*...

I lower my head, ashamed at where my imagination is taking me. I don't want to hurt my wife. And yet, a small part of me deep down inside is raging to be let loose. To explore our boundaries. To try something, *anything*, new, until we fully discover our limits.

I hear the delicate rattle of the chain as she finally drops it from her mouth. Her head is still lowered when she lifts one of her hands to cover mine as it grips the handle of the paddle. "Do it," she says, squeezing tight. Her voice is low and it vibrates with some kind of emotion that I don't quite get. This is *Grace*, and yet, it's not. *My* Grace doesn't sound like this, all sexy and sultry and begging for pain.

"I love you, darling. You know that. We don't have to—"

"Do it!" Her tone is almost vicious in its intensity.

Do it? "Grace, you don't understand. What if..." I pound my chest with my other fist tightly clenched, even though she can't see me in this position. "I'm *afraid* of what's in here."

"Henry." She shakes her head, and the movement must do something to the pressure of the clips as a yelp chokes out of her.

"You want them off?"

"Fuck no." Her voice is husky. "I trust you. Spank me right *there*. I deserve it. I need it."

I close my eyes. *She trusts you. Trust yourself.*

I position myself and she wriggles her acceptance, trying to ease her pussy lips around me. When I penetrate her it feels smooth and natural, the juices from both of us flowing so freely there is no resistance whatsoever. Her channel closes around my hard flesh, hot and wet and tight, and I thrust a couple of times, seating myself as deeply as I can.

I center the leather padding right up against her clit. Then I strike, hard, opening my eyes again at the moment of impact, just in time to see her lurch beneath me and hear the agonized scream that forces its way out of her throat.

CHAPTER 5

GRACE

My nipples are already on fire, and when he spanks me this time the pain is so intense it ricochets from my clit right through my whole body and back again. Even my fingertips ache. The scream bursts out involuntarily. I can't help it; the agony is seated right there in my core. I hate it. Yet I also love it, this delicate balance between pleasure and pain that creates a power all its own. It takes away thought and reduces my calculated reasoning to nothing, until my boundaries are gone and all I can do is *feel*.

He lashes out again so suddenly I'm not prepared and another squeal leaves my lips at the smarting sting across my mound. The pain is different to what it felt like on my buttocks. So sharp and real that instant tears brim up and over. I like it on my ass. The pain reverberates deep and is somewhat cushioned by my flesh. I'm forty next month. I have a lot of flesh in that area, these days. But across my pussy? Right on my clit? And with these nipple clamps on… The sensation is much more concentrated, less able to be diffused.

Our safe word floats through my mind and I'm tempted,

but before I can speak he pauses and indulgent fingers caress down my spine. "Okay?" His tone is concerned, loving, and in that moment I know for sure he will never hurt me the way I was hurt in the past.

"I'm good." Tears spurt again, blurring my vision, but this time they stem from the knowledge that I'm loved, and that he will never take me further than I need. "Not as hard, please. Don't stop though. Please, don't stop."

The spanking starts up again, gentler this time, and he moves inside me in rhythm with his strokes, thrusting back and forth in a fast and slippery embrace with my cunt. The bite of his disciplinary action, and the plunging movement deep within my body, occur almost simultaneously and now the sounds that are coming out of my mouth don't even sound human anymore. I think my whimpering goads him even further and suddenly he's riding me as if there's no tomorrow. His free arm, not the one holding the paddle, slides around my waist to bind us tightly together. He's all hard muscle and soft skin. Such a contradiction, and yet it matches perfectly.

His erection is massive, filling me so completely that I can't differentiate between what is pain and what is pleasure any more. My whole body is throbbing, the blood pounding through my veins, and I don't know how much more I can take. I am crying, screaming, and falling apart, and I know it is building again toward orgasm, and this time everything is so much deeper and more intense. I can't do this... I can't... I'm just about to shout "yellow" when he stops spanking me and drops the paddle.

"No more." His voice is shaking. "I call time." I can't do anything but kneel here and sob while he loosens the clamps, removing them one at a time. The pain crescendos even higher for a brief moment as the blood rushes back into the pinched flesh. Eventually it begins to ease, my muscles start to relax, and my head drops to one side, silently inviting his kiss.

I need gentle now. Not harsh.

Henry complies as if he knows exactly what I want, and this time his lips and tongue do connect with my skin in a move that is both familiar and strange. He is masterful, strong, and more sure than usual, and my eyes close in delight at the sensations that spread outward from where his mouth works at my neck. No confusion about this response. His mouth on my neck is pure pleasure, and I relax fully beneath him as his kiss deepens.

"Darling," he murmurs, and my heart almost bursts at the tenderness contained in his voice. "I love you." His words vibrate against my neck and it's as if his love is trying to crawl right inside to hold me tight in its embrace.

"I love you, too, Henry." My eyes are wet yet again, and this time it isn't an out-of-control raging of my emotions that drives the tears, only the quiet dampness that comes from a deep-seated happiness. I feel him slide out of me and the emptiness is a shock. "No! I want you back inside me."

"I will be. Soon. First I need you to lie down, and roll over to face me."

He's the master, tonight, so I do as he says and when I see how much love there is in his gaze I have to look away for fear of drowning in the emotion. Turning my head brings me in direct view of his erection. From this angle it looks even bigger than usual, his balls tightly drawn up, and I ache to touch that silken heat. He hasn't given permission, though, and I don't want to incite more punishment right now. Everything hurts and I'm not sure I can take any more pain.

He must read whatever mute message is visible in my face. He hesitates, looking away from me toward his bag of toys, and then a rueful grin twists his lips. Whatever his intention was, it coalesces back into what I need right now. He leans down, his arm muscles flexing as he takes his own weight, and dips his tongue into that most private place between my legs. The moist heat of his mouth as he kisses and licks me there is soothing and yet arousing, both at the same time, as if he is trying to make up for what went before by sucking the pain away.

"Oh yes, Henry, that feels so good. Keep—*oh*!"

He nips at my clit, very gently, and then his tongue swirls around the sensitive bud, licking and sucking hard. The pain from my spanking is still there, but only as background heat. This intense ache centered in my cunt has nothing to do with pain and everything to do with desire. A moan escapes me, and I sink my fingers into his dark hair, urging him on. I lift one of my legs up and over his shoulder, my foot resting behind him on the edge of the couch, and the access is obviously better. He works his way further along my seam, holding my labia lips apart to lap at the delicate flesh beneath. My breathing is harsh and heavy, and in the quiet of the cottage the ragged noise stands out even above the pop and crackle of fire in the grate, and Henry's moist licking noises as he finally breaches my channel with a hot stab of his tongue.

Is it his tongue? Maybe it's a finger. I can't tell. The whole area is on fire and all I can do is shake and quiver and pray that he's nearly ready, because I'm about to explode right there against his mouth. His tender ministrations take me right back to the edge, and again I feel the beginnings of an exquisite climax clutching at my womb. In an instant he's there above me, re-entering me with a cock so thick and hard I know it can only be moments before he climaxes, too.

I wrap my legs around his hips, holding him tight. Urging him deeper.

"This time we come together." His voice is heavy, shaking, and I reach up to cup his face.

I love *this man. I love him.*

He stills above me before suddenly thrusting hard, and his breathing loses all rhythm. "Love you." His gasping words are hoarse and I know we're about to go over the edge together.

"I love you too," I manage, and then we're gone as my channel begins to clench violently around his shaft, trying to milk my husband of every last drop of his cum. I'm sucking his juices into me and making them mine. *Mine*! He groans loudly, his whole body shuddering as he gives himself to me, and beneath him I continue to buck crazily as we orgasm together in an escape that seems to go on forever.

Space and time cease to exist, and I'm drifting without thought, until a delicate caress runs down my side. It's too firm to be his fingers. I think it might be the edge of the paddle. "Not yet, Henry," I murmur. "It's too soon." I can't do it again right now. I just want to continue laying here with him, our limbs tangled together and our arms circled tight around each other while the fire pops and crackles and keeps the darkness at bay.

His laughter shakes us both. With a smooth movement he pulls out of me and we lie together on our sides, facing one another. He is still chuckling as he reaches out to trace the line of my jaw. It feels wonderful, with the heat of the fire warming my back and his touch creating pimpled goose bumps wherever his fingers trail along my curves.

"Even *I* can't get it up again that quickly, Gracie."

"Oh. Sure. I knew that."

He leans in and kisses me on the lips, a slow and gentle gesture, and this close I can see the faint lines that fan out from his eyes. I trace them, wondering if the stress of our living a lie for so long has added to their depths, and then his eyes crinkle up at the corners as he grins, turning a negative into a positive. My husband's wrinkles are beautiful. They show his true depth of character.

"Any regrets?"

I consider his question for a moment. *Regrets? Lots of them. Most of all...* "I wish I'd let us be ourselves a long time ago. If only I'd been—"

"Grace." He covers my mouth with a firm finger, silencing more words. "We have a whole lifetime still ahead of us, to live our lives as we wish. Whether we make this a regular thing, and book a remote holiday cottage a couple of times a year—"

"Only a couple of times?"

A dark brow rises upward. "Well, as often as you want, then."

I laugh. "Maybe we should go see the bank. Look at taking out a loan to buy a little holiday shack."

He smooths wayward hair out of my eyes and smiles back at me. "I think that's a damn good idea, Gracie. This may have been our first time, but it's definitely not going to be our last."

I look across toward the overnight bag he brought with him and a surge of light-heartedness runs through me. "That's a very big bag you have, Henry. A couple of nipple clamps and a spanking paddle can't possibly take up all that space."

I arch my brow and wait for his response, and he doesn't disappoint. "Hmm, seems as if maybe I *can* get it up again that quickly, after all." His erection surges to life against my belly, inciting an answering ache deep inside me. "I have lots of exciting toys yet to show you, babe. Our play time is only just beginning."

His kiss this time is deep, not quite as gentle, and I sense the mastery that he's kept hidden all this time coming to the fore. I can't wait. "Bring it on then, Sir. I'm ready. For you. For us. For our future."

The End

I hope you enjoyed MARRIAGE GAMES. Want more in the FORBIDDEN series? Keep reading for ALPHA SUBMISSIVE.

ALPHA SUBMISSIVE

A BONDAGE ROMANCE

PREFACE

When a driven, alpha woman is forced by circumstance to participate in a shibari rope display, her inner submissive is unleashed in ways she never imagined possible.

Shibari Master Roane is the epitome of "alpha", but when his assistant can no longer work their world-class suspension show, his eye turns toward the woman who hired him for her avant-garde BDSM festival.

Ava only agreed to run the festival in memory of her late, emotionally-damaged brother. If she steps in as surrogate model for this expert suspension rigger, will her demons remain hidden behind the alpha wall she's managed to erect, or will Roane use his rope like an extension of those sexy fingers to strip away every protection until nothing is left, but Ava's naked truth?

CHAPTER ONE

"Your model might be expecting a baby?" I struggle to draw in oxygen as I process what Roane has just told me. "And she's still in hospital?" Throwing up your guts several times a day is a legitimate way for someone to get out of a shibari session. I guess. But I booked this world-renowned rope bondage team months ago, and their performance is scheduled to be held in front of an international crowd of guests and visiting media in only three days' time.

Well, hell. One more problem to add to the growing list. How am I going to fix this?

I take a deliberate slow breath, hoping to convince my heart rate to head back down to somewhere near normal. Then I realize what I haven't actually said. "Oh. Congratulations to you both." I sound churlish and I don't want to, but in my wildest dreams I simply can't imagine the rope Master leaning casually against my office wall in the role of an expectant dad. *My* rope Master. At least, he's supposed to be for the next week or so, until the Avant-garde lifestyle festival I'm in charge of is over and I can finally get some rest.

Who am I kidding? I can't remember what R&R feels

like, anymore. For the first time in its five-year history, this festival has caught the attention of the international media, thanks to the reputation of the bondage expert standing across from me, and I haven't had more than three or four hours sleep a night for weeks.

I lean forward, clenching my hands together on the desk when I notice the tremble in my fingers. I know its stress, but it's damn annoying. Last week got so bad I finally visited my doctor but she just told me what I already know. *"Cut yourself some slack, Ava. If you keep going at this pace you'll make yourself seriously ill. I know you made a promise to your brother to keep his festival going, but—"* I raised my hand and cut her off at that point, not wanting to hear the rest. Her words won't bring Connor back. And resting won't help me get things done for this blasted event that seems to have taken over my life.

Since that visit, the muscle tremors have gotten worse. It irks me beyond belief that I can't control my bodily responses. *Don't show weakness to anyone.* That's what Dad said to Connor and me, over and over when we were kids. *If you do they'll find a way to exploit it.* We never knew who "they" were, but it was drummed into us so often that we both tucked away our weaknesses where no one else could find them.

Last year it all became too much for my twin brother and... *No. Don't think about that now.* I frown at my traitorous hands, then lift my eyes to the man in front of me, giving him my best executive stare.

"Your show is the keynote performance, Roane. A baby is wonderful news and I'm pleased for you both, of course. It's a shame Nicole is unwell enough to be hospitalized, but at least she's getting the right care. Surely—"

"It's not mine."

I blink at the blunt statement. "Sorry, I just assumed—"

"Everyone does. Nicole and I don't have that kind of relationship. She's my public shibari model, but that's as far as it goes. She's married."

Oh. My brows descend again. How can that be? Nicole, who happens to be slim and beautiful, is naked when they perform, Roane partially so, and quite frankly he's the sexiest man I've ever met in my life. How could there *not* be some kind of chemistry or spark between them? "Well, um, surely you have someone else you can call on to step in? Someone in the lifestyle, perhaps, who likes being, you know…tied up?"

My voice trails off and I lose my train of thought in the intensity of his gaze. No one has that effect on me. *Ever.* And yet here I am, drowning in the depths of his stare and wondering what it would feel like to be tightly bound and completely at the mercy of a man like Roane.

He's a strange hybrid mix of race that I can't quite pinpoint, and unlike anyone I've ever met. His build is tall and lean rather than overly-muscled, with tanned skin and almost black hair cut short at the back and sides. His nose is bordering on too strong and his mouth is wide, with a definite hint of sardonic in the way it lifts at one corner whenever he listens to me speak. His eyes tilt up slightly at the outer corners, and the green of his irises is so intense it reminds me of the fragrant mint my assistant grows in a little tub on the windowsill of our office kitchenette.

Roane is not classically handsome at all, and yet there's something about him that is so compelling, I can't tear my gaze away when he enters the room. Neither can anyone else, I've noticed. It's as if he's found a way to bottle whatever makes a man "alpha," and then sprayed himself liberally with the heady scent. Every cell in my body wakes up the moment he's in my vicinity, and even when I try not to think about what he does for a living, my mind slips immediately to a place where I imagine those long, strong fingers working diligently to bind me into submission with a series of intricate, unbreakable knots.

I clear my throat, trying unsuccessfully to break this hypnotic spell he seems to weave. The thought of handing over that much control...complete and utter control...to someone else...and especially to *him*...

A shiver traverses my skin and sends a strong signal straight to my clit. I don't understand the sudden aching throb between my legs. This gig was Connor's, not mine, and I'm only in the driver seat of this festival because I made him a promise last year before he passed away. The BDSM lifestyle isn't one I've ever been particularly drawn to, and even though my brother seemed to get enormous satisfaction from his role as a sub, it isn't something I've considered for myself.

If Roane ever tries to tie *me* up the way he does to that poor woman, I'd probably have a hissy fit. I'm not that sort of woman. He knows it, and so do I.

Again that betraying pulse of need makes itself felt, as if my body is calling out my mind as a blatant liar. I clench my thighs in an effort to control it, but that only intensifies the sensation and I know there is wetness pooling now in my overheated pussy.

His eyes are amused as he stares at me, and I wonder if he's aware of his arousing effect. Probably. His lips twitch, doing that sardonic curl. Definitely then. *Bastard*.

I stare back, trying not to be intimidated even though my nipples begin to harden in an unsolicited confirmation of the burgeoning lust staking its claim on my body.

"No." His voice is cool but his eyes are still hot with laughter, and my brain shuts down for a moment.

What are we talking about? "No, what?"

He's wearing a black T-shirt, black jeans, and boots. The outfit shows off his lean physique and muscled arms and shoulders, and my heart skips a beat at the thought of those same muscles rippling with effort as he hoists the rope rigging during one of his shows. *What would it feel like, to be bound, and then suspended by an expert rigger?*

He raises a brow, then answers with exaggerated patience. "No, there is unlikely to be anyone else available at this short notice." He pushes off the wall with one shoulder and walks toward me, and once again my breath is temporarily trapped in the base of my lungs. Roane moves with a measured precision that is the opposite of flamboyant, and yet every action is all the more intriguing because of its very restraint. His quiet stillness is so innate that when he moves it seems more profound, more *noticeable*, than when others do the same.

It takes effort to concentrate on our conversation, especially when he grips the back of my visitor's chair with those strong hands, and then leans close, only centimeters away. His fresh, understated aroma wafts across my nostrils in a tantalizing hint of clean masculinity. I can't tell if he's wearing aftershave, or if that heady, slightly woodsy scent is just part of who he is. Either way he smells delicious and when I inhale I have to consciously stop myself from letting out a pleasurable groan.

"What would you suggest, then?" Now I sound ridiculous, like a breathy schoolgirl with a crush on her teacher.

"I'll put out a call to my contacts," he says. "But suspension sessions involve an enormous level of trust and commitment from each of the parties. It can be dangerous if not done correctly, and there's more chance for things to go wrong if the model and the rigger have no real connection. Other than Nicole, there are very few people I would be willing to put in that position."

I slump in the chair, disappointment forcing my mind back onto the job as I try to figure out what we can do to salvage this. *Oh, Connor.* My brother worked so hard, and now I'm right on the cusp of achieving the level of acclaim he craved. If we can just get Roane to cooperate.

When he shifts, I flinch a little. The question that follows drops into the room and lays there between us like a poisonous snake. "Why don't *you* do it, Ava?"

A bark of laughter escapes and the mesmerizing effect is finally broken. "Nope. Not going to happen, Roane. I'm sorry, but you'll just *have* to find someone else."

"We have a connection already. I've known that ever since you saw my performance in New York."

He feels it too? I can't deny there's *something* between us, but to take the leap from being aware of each other sexually, to participating in a public shibari session with one of the world's most well-respected Dominants…

I'm already shaking my head but he just looks at me, and I feel like a twelve-year old who's been caught out in bad behaviour. Suddenly I'm babbling, the bubble of anxiety rising. "I can't, Roane. There's no way. You must know I don't have a submissive bone in my body. I wouldn't even know how to—"

"There *is* no one else. It's you, or I cancel." Again, his voice is quiet, but it carries an edge of steel that sends awareness shivering down my spine. He means it. If he cancels, the festival will be ruined, and with it my late brother's reputation.

"Look." I speak in a firm yet calm tone, aiming for reason. "Let's consider this for a minute. Your show sold out within an hour of tickets going on sale. We have media from seven countries here just to see you. *Seven*, Roane. It would destroy our reputation if you cancel. *Please…*"

I bite my lip to stop the desperate begging before it really gets started. Connor and Dad would have been shaking their heads in disbelief to see me like this. *I'm letting them down.* I want to burst into tears, but crying is a useless waste of energy. Another of Dad's famous sayings. Instead, I do what I always do when tears threaten, and mentally give myself a slap. *Okay, Ava, get your act together. Stay tough, and get things sorted.*

His head tilts to one side and I can see he's caught the movement of my teeth attacking my bottom lip. He looks more interested than he should, and I stop biting. *Friggin' anxiety. I hate it.*

"It's one performance," he says after a pause. "You could wear a blindfold for much of it, and we can get you a wig if it makes you more comfortable. No one will even know it's you." While he talks he releases one hand from the back of the chair and I follow the gesture of those long fingers back and forth. I wish he didn't sound so reasonable. It makes me feel like I should seriously consider his suggestion.

I'm hesitating, on the verge of arguing some more, when he adds, "And you're wrong about one thing, Ava. There's a part of you that *craves* submission. You just don't know it yet, because no one has ever shown you properly how to tap into that part of yourself."

Submission. The word sends a prickle across my skin and I shiver again, but not with cold. It's something unfamiliar at my core that is suddenly fighting hard to get out. It terrifies and excites me, all in the same moment.

What the hell is this man's secret? He binds women so tightly with rope that he has to keep checking throughout the show to make sure their fingers and toes don't drop off from lack of circulation. In the end they can't move a muscle, and when he hoists them up to show them off as art, people don't call him a sadist. Rather, they call him an artist and flock to see his work.

On a sensible, rational level none of that appeals to me. I don't want to have my humanity stripped bare and be reborn simply as an object of art. Completely at someone else's mercy. I *don't*. So, what is it about this dominant male that makes me forget everything sensible, and sets off these strange cravings that are growing so strong they fill my belly with crazed flip-flopping agitation?

Roane. What would it be like to have your hard cock buried deep inside me while you stare down with those intense green eyes? Would you hold still while I come, or would you thrust so deep in my cunt that I'd have no choice but to explode around your organ? What would it be like to have those fingers caress the slit between my legs until an orgasm takes me to a place where I can forget everything and everyone?

What would it be like, if you did all that while I was bound and unable to move?

I can't believe I've descended to this in my imagination, and yet my sex is slippery with cream as my thoughts continue to run wild. I know that if I stand up right now there'll be a wet patch on my seat. Thank God for these tailored black trousers, and the ability to slide my chair closer to the desk to hide my faithless response.

"I met your brother several times."

Well. Didn't see that one coming. "I didn't know that."

"I considered him a friend. I *know* your family history, Ava. Your dad's gone now. He's two thousand miles away in Perth, and he's not coming back to Melbourne. He wouldn't dare show his face here again. He's finally out of your life for good. You don't have to be strong and tough every waking moment in an effort to try and stand up to him. For yourself, *or* for Connor. Not anymore."

My hand is at my mouth and I can't think straight. "How—"

"He was a *bully*, Ava. I'm a Dominant, one of the best, and when you submit to me there will be an enormous difference in your experience."

I open and close my mouth, wanting to applaud him for his persuasive skills, but my heart is pounding so fast I'm afraid I'll have a heart attack. I'm losing control over the crazy thing deep inside. Is it panic? Maybe. Whatever it is, it's hammering for release.

Yes. Do it. Try it. Just the once. You know you need what he's offering.

"For a few hours on Saturday night, you will hand over responsibility to another person. To *me*. And what you will experience, Ava, is complete and cathartic release. I promise you won't regret your decision."

I swallow, trying to force the lump of panic back down. *Sure. I'll be completely safe, in front of a massive crowd, with the world's media watching on to make sure I don't get hurt...*

"We will have a practice run on Friday. Just you and me at my apartment here in Melbourne. No audience. After that, if you say no, I'll honor your wish. Would that make you feel better?"

"Maybe." *Just you and me, and a slithery rope? In your apartment? Hell no, that will not make me feel any better!*

The crazy thing lurches. It feels like a serious attack of the butterflies. Heck, forget butterflies. This feels more like a stampede of wild animals. My vagina clenches and my clit is so swollen it aches. I'm having trouble sitting still. Again I clamp my thighs, but that only heightens the effect as my labia lips glide against one another, flesh on creamy flesh.

So much wetness there between my legs. How long has it been since I've felt any kind of sexual desire whatsoever? Too long. But here, in front of Roane, with the offer to visit his apartment for a private one-on-one shibari session? The urge to slip my hand between my legs and start masturbating is almost overwhelming.

I unclench my fingers and flex them experimentally on the desktop, stunned to discover the tremor has subsided. I cannot believe what I'm about to say next, and yet my body is already celebrating the words with another involuntary clench of vaginal muscle. "I'll…consider it."

Roane grins, showing a flash of neat white teeth, and the action reminds me of a tiger who has just spotted its prey. *Danger*. "Yes, Ava, by all means. *Consider* it."

CHAPTER TWO

I don't think I can do this. In fact, I'm positive I can't.

I chose to wear my old flannel robe because it is thick and comforting, but standing here in the middle of his Melbourne studio apartment, looking up at a convoluted rope pulley suspension system, is about as far from comfortable as I can imagine. There's a lone seat that looks somewhat like a park bench, situated in the middle of a large square-shaped room, and I wonder if I'm supposed to sit there. Or just stand up? Or…

What the heck am I supposed to do? If he doesn't get here soon I'm going to pass out from hyper-ventilating.

When I finally agreed to give this a try, I knew he would expect me to be naked, but the reality of that is so much harder to deal with than an abstract concept. Naked? Sure. During my shower this morning I shaved everything to within an inch of its life, moisturized all over, and squirted perfume in unfamiliar places. All the while this strange mix of fear and excitement fought a war within my system.

Except…now that I'm standing here with my clothing stacked in a neat pile in his bathroom next door, fear seems to be winning out. This robe isn't nearly thick enough to keep me modest, especially when I'm completely naked underneath it, *and* alone with him in his home.

I rub my sweaty hands on the robe, trying to focus on what's around me. *Concentrate, damn it. There's no need to be this scared. You're tough.*

Wide polished floorboards line the room, beneath a thick, burgundy-colored rug in the center. One wall is completely mirrored from floor to ceiling, while the others are draped with a black velvety-looking fabric that creates a cozy, almost closed-in effect. The rigging system built into the ceiling houses a series of down lights as well as a bunch of cables and heck knows what else. The result is like a cross between a dance studio and a decadent bedroom—only there's no bed, just that unusual bench seat with a black wrought-iron back, and along one of the fabric-draped walls there's a heavy wooden sideboard with a series of cupboards.

One thing I do like in this room is the lighting. For some reason I expected glaring white theatre lights, but it is actually golden and not at all stark. When I catch a glimpse of my anxious face in the mirror, I can see the warmth of that light softening my reflection and giving my brown hair interesting chestnut highlights.

"Ava." His voice is a caress and a command, all contained in that one word. I automatically pull the robe tighter around me as I turn toward him. He's standing in the doorway, but already his presence seems to fill the room. He's dominant in the truest sense of the word. When he's around, no one else matters. But I'm dominant too. Aren't I?

I raise my chin and give him a look. The one that makes everyone in the office sit up and take notice when I speak. I add in a small smile, trying to soften the effect a little, but still wanting to remind him that he doesn't own me—I'm only here under sufferance.

"I have no idea how this is going to work, Roane. I won't hand over control. It's not in me to do that." The crazy thing tucked away inside starts laughing.

Liar, liar. Just you wait and see.

One eyebrow lifts as he studies me, and when he doesn't smile back mine slowly disappears. "Remove your robe." *Hmm. Foreplay, anyone?* Making internal jokes to stave off the panic doesn't seem to be working. My chest heaves as I suck in a deep breath and let it out slowly, debating whether or not to argue. But what would be the point? I'm the one that agreed to this, and I'm here to do a job.

Baring myself to him physically is hard, but it's doable. I might be rusty in the sexual stakes, but I'm not a complete novice. What is hidden deep down inside is what scares me more, but as long as I stay in control of my emotions I'll be fine. *Okay. I can do this.*

I do as he commands, my hands fumbling, making what I'm sure is a ridiculous spectacle as I finally untie the belt and let the robe drop to the floor. I step over the messy puddle of flannel pooling around my feet and wait for what comes next.

What does he think? Is he regretting this already? I'm not thin, and I'm not that young anymore, either. I turned thirty-five just over a month ago, and I've been too busy lately to look after myself properly. I've been eating a lot of take-out and it probably shows on my waist and hips.

In that instant I realize that I *want* him to like me; to desire me in the same way my body seems to crave his. The urge to weep comes over me, but I refuse to give in to it. As he moves further into the room and circles me, I find myself wishing that I were the type of woman who might truly attract a man like Roane.

I imagine someone beautiful. Perhaps a pale blonde like Nicole to counter his darkness, with a slender, youthful frame and a come-hither flirtiness in her gaze. He would love that. My plain brown hair, freckled nose, and larger-than-average build must be a huge let-down.

Finally I can't stand the silence. "Look, I'm probably not…" He continues to circle, studying me as if I'm a creature at the zoo. It's like he's trying to memorize every dip and curve of my body, drinking in the sight of me with those intense green eyes, and I swallow hard and try again. "I'm probably not quite what you're used to. Nicole was stunning, I know. I only met her the once, but—"

"Quiet." The word slices across my nervous babble. He brings his hand up to his chin, rubbing it a couple of times and frowning in seeming concentration. "Your curves are just right for what I have in mind." Suddenly the frown is gone and he nods decisively. "Yes. I see it. The patterns are becoming clear." He leans close and touches my collarbone, running his finger lightly along the contoured ridge and stopping at the dip in my throat. "This is going to work out just fine."

His finger flutters down toward the curve of my breast but it is gone before it reaches the nipple. I don't know why, but it is as if I can still feel his hand on me, warm and firm, continuing its run over the swell of my flesh. A line of goose bumps forms in the wake of an imaginary touch rimming my nipple, and I let out a tiny hiss. *How can you make me feel such things when you didn't even touch me there?*

"You're beautiful, too, Ava." He nods toward my pale face in the mirror. "I know you don't believe that, but I see it. And in this room, *I* am the Master."

I study my reflection but I don't see anything beautiful about my curves. My body is stiff with tension and my hands are clenched by my side. I shake my head, then shrug, trying to release some of the tightness across my shoulder muscles. "I've been called strong before. Capable. *Annoying*, at times." I let out a light laugh, trying for casual. "Even bitchy. But beautiful? I've never been called that. Before now." I didn't mean to add that last bit. It sounds fragile and weak. The involuntary exposure annoys me.

He touches my shoulder and I turn from our reflections to face him. There is pity in his eyes, and I hate it, but there is something else behind the pity that has my heart racing even faster and sends an aching pulse directly to my core. *Desire.* The knowledge claws at my system and tears my hesitation to shreds.

"All righty then. Let's do this, Roane."

"No, Ava. From this point *I'm* in control. Not you."

My lips part, but before I can say anything further he pushes me down onto the bench seat. "*Now* we will start."

"Wait. Um…" My mouth is dry. "Don't we need a safe word, or…something?" My voice fades at the amusement that animates his features.

"You could always say *stop*." He crosses the room to the sideboard and retrieves several long sections of rope from one of the cupboards. Is he still amused? I can't tell. "We don't need a safe word as such, unless you want one. Rope bondage is inherently unsafe, but I know what I'm doing." He shrugs. "Better than almost anyone, of course." His self-confidence borders on arrogance and yet I know he's correct. He *is* a Master. "I will check on you regularly. Your circulation. Your well-being. You must answer me when I ask, but I trust that you will. Do you trust that I will do the right thing by *you*, Ava?"

Do *I trust him? He's the world's best. I've seen his work.*

Something in me relaxes just a touch. "Yes. I do trust you." *As much as I can ever trust anyone.*

"Good. Now back to your safe word. What would you like it to be?"

He *is* still laughing at me, and my mind goes blank. I can't think of a single word. He looks like a predator, watching and waiting, ready to pounce, and I finally blurt out, "Tiger."

His mouth quirks, but then his shoulders lift in capitulation. "Tiger. Sure. Use that word if you want to pause or end our game. At any time." He grins then, with a feral cast to his features that only enhances his similarity to the animal in question. "But you won't."

CHAPTER THREE

He starts with my wrists, wrapping them several times and then creating an intricate knot that sort of folds back on itself. He calls that first one a double-column tie. He continues to wrap, and even though my hands are positioned in front rather than behind and I make an effort to study what he does, I have no idea how those knots work. Even if I did, with my wrists bound together like this I have no chance of getting any of it undone.

The other end of the rope disappears up toward that pulley system near the ceiling, but at this point I'm still seated. My anxiety continues to lurk in the wings, and when he re-positions my arms in a type of prayer pose in front of my breasts and then casts a couple of larger loops around my torso, the apprehension kicks into overdrive. One of my usual coping mechanisms is to breathe slow and deep, but the loops around my chest are quite close-fitting and when my breathing starts to escalate the restriction becomes uncomfortable.

My throat is tight, and a tiny moan escapes. *Why am I*

doing this? What do I really know about him? What if he wraps me so tight I can't breathe? What if... I don't think I can... Oh, my God...

"You're doing fine, Ava. Let it out."

Let *what* out?

"Focus on the rope. What does it feel like against your skin?"

Okay. I can do this. I'm strong. The rope. Focus on the rope.

I expect it to be scratchy against my skin, but it isn't. Instead, the rope glides over the contours of my body like the caressing fingers of a lover whose sole purpose is to provide pleasure for his partner. Roane is clearly a Master. I remind myself he's had lots of practice, but it doesn't stop the trail of goose bumps forming in the wake of the silken strands and though I fight to control it, a shudder wracks my body as the sensation wends its way once again to my traitorous clit.

"It feels...pleasurable."

"Yes. Let it out, Ava."

The only thing that wants out is my panic, and I refuse to give in. I shake my head violently but the rope is there again, together with the exciting brush of his fingertips as he weaves some kind of intricate pattern around my body. I love his fingers on my skin. They are warm, and firm, and the gentle touch mirrors the exciting feel of that cord slithering over my limbs and then pulling taut as he fastens it around me. I'm panting a bit and it's starting to get painful. The rope. It's so *tight*...

I press my lips together, trying to contain my emotions, but the anxiety is ballooning as fast as my desire and the breathlessness increases.

"I'm not sure... I'm not sure..."

He pauses and in the silence it's as if I can hear my own heartbeat pounding in my ears. Fast. Staccato. Out of control.

"Do you want to use your safe word?"

Yes. No. I shake my head. These two warring factions inside my body are tearing me apart, and yet another of my coping mechanisms has been taken away. Instead of the freedom to pace back and forth across my office, giving me precious minutes to tamp my emotions back down, I'm now tethered to that damn pulley ring attached to the ceiling, and I can hardly move at all.

Another moan forces its way out of my throat, and Roane's hand immediately cups my naked ass. He strokes me there, as if calming a skittish kitten, and while the anxiety decreases a little my desire ramps up, throwing everything out of balance. I start laughing, wondering if he knows just how close I am to the edge, but he presses a finger to my lips.

"Shh. You're doing well, Ava."

Am I? How would I know? The only time I've ever seen a shibari performance was when I visited a lifestyle festival in New York several months ago to find out why Connor had insisted on booking this particular rigger. *Roane.* They all talk about him with reverence, whispering his name as if he's some kind of demi-god in the field of BDSM. I went there prepared to roll my eyes and ridicule. I discovered a man who took my breath away from the very first second I saw him, and witnessed a display that populated my thoughts, and my dreams, long after I returned home.

He's good. More than good. His concentration and skilled precision is utterly fascinating. As I looked around the room that day I saw avid intensity mixed with awed respect on the faces of everyone in that audience. My face probably reflected the same.

Connor was right. Roane *is* a Dominant. And right now that Dom is reaching between my legs to feed a loop of rope along my moist seam and up over my clit. Just the thought of his hand down there makes me hover on the precipice of an orgasm. The nub poking out from my labia is so swollen and sensitized that when he pulls gently, making a tiny adjustment to the lay of the cord, I can't contain an intense shudder that wracks my whole body from head to toe.

I catch his satisfied smirk and strangely, it enhances my excitement. So he's a man after all, not a machine, and part of him must enjoy turning me on. It's not all about making me submit. His cock has grown hard as he continues to wrap me. I can see the outline of his bulge tenting those dark trousers, and it's an impressive size. I don't remember him being aroused like that during the session I watched with Nicole as his model. I would have noticed, I'm sure. The moment he appeared on stage I was more aware of his presence—every nuance of expression, every move, every breath—than I've ever been of anyone.

Even back then, before I officially met him backstage after the show, there was part of me that recognized and celebrated Roane's effect on my system. His influence was so compelling that I dreamed for several nights after that event of his hands, his lengths of rope, encircling my body like a strange cocoon offering warmth and security.

During the day I dismissed the dreams as ridiculous fantasies. But at night…

The memory of those New York dreams, and the many that have followed since I returned to Melbourne, invades my mind and a fresh rush of cream releases from my vagina. I want to growl with the frustration of not being able to move. Not being able to touch myself to relieve the growing pressure of arousal.

I ache to reach out and unzip his trousers. Is he circumcised beneath that fabric? I have no idea where he is originally from, so I can't even guess based on heritage or culture. All I know is that he maintains three homes—one each in Melbourne, New York, and Tokyo—and that his shibari performance and workshop services are in such high demand that he is estimated to be worth a small fortune.

As he moves back and forth around me I catch tantalizing glimpses of his hard-on. What would he do if I darted my head forward and nipped at his erection? Would he punish me with even tighter restraints? I'm so tempted to give it a try. I want to lower that zipper with my teeth and watch the turgid flesh spring free, and then lean over to take him fully into my mouth and sample his exotic flavor. But I'm helpless, bound by these rope shackles.

The frustration bursts out of me. "What do you need me to do, Roane? Please. Tell me."

He lets out a little snort. "Nothing. Whilst you are in this session, *I* am in charge of everything."

"But—"

"Stop talking." His admonishment is quiet, but once again I detect that steel edge in his tone. He adjusts a line of rope running beneath my breasts, and then his fingers graze one of my nipples, ever so gently. For some reason it stops my breath altogether. It's not the rope. It's his touch. I want to feel it again. I *need* to feel it again. Why does the lightest of touches on my breast send a message directly to my sex?

"What is the rope made of? I thought it would be jute or something. Rough."

He sighs then; one that sounds like a long-suffering parent stuck with a petulant child. I know he wants me to be quiet, but I *have* to talk. If I can't move, how else will I maintain control?

He's moving, circling me again, and I shift my head back and forth, trying to figure out where he is and what he's planning next. Is he close? Is he standing back, studying my form and working out where his next loop is likely to go? Does he like what he sees when he looks at me? My anxiety begins to escalate again, and I'm trying desperately to hold it in when his warm breath tickles my ear. "It's made of soft cotton. Not my usual choice, but it's perfect for a beginner like you." His voice is low, with a touch of wry amusement underlying the words. "It's non-slip. And machine-washable. Great for things like *this*."

His touch on my pussy is feather-light as he strokes the whole length of my seam with the end of yet another piece of rope. Again a spurt of wetness escapes my channel. *Oh my God, did he see the fluid come out that time?* I try to shift my legs more tightly together, but his firm grip stops me. He runs his hand from my inner thigh down one leg to my ankle and grasps firmly, bending my leg until my calf hits the back of my thigh. This position pulls my leg sideways and my pussy is almost fully exposed except for that one line of rope embedded along the slit. He binds my bent leg once, twice, and then a third time, with a look of intense concentration as he works to secure the loop.

He's totally involved in this, whereas I, despite my arousal, still retain a sense of disengagement. I'm enduring it, waiting for the session to be over so I can move freely and have full control over my own body once again.

He looks up from his crouched position beside me, and I lose myself in the brilliant depths of his gaze. I could *drown* in those pools of emerald. "This won't work for either of us unless you commit." There's a thread of annoyance in his tone and the urge to placate him fills me. But then he says it again. "Let it out."

"Let *what* out, for fuck's sake?"

Pity shimmers within the green. "You *know*, Ava."

"I don't." *Don't pity me, Roane. Please. Don't pity me.* "I can't."

CHAPTER FOUR

Perhaps my silent plea is visible in my eyes. Perhaps he sees the betraying tremble of my chin as I fight to stay in control. I don't know what drives him to suddenly reach out and caress my jawline. It's the most loving gesture I've ever felt and it is almost my undoing. I look past him, up toward the ceiling, biting at my lip and trying not to blink until those damn tears are absorbed back into my eyes.

When he touches me again it's not on my face, and I yelp at the unexpected shock of his thumb sliding beneath the cord to rub my clit, back and forth several times. My legs, one free, one bent and bound, involuntarily slide open wider to give him easier access. My whole body is betraying my brain, it seems.

"You're so wet," he says, and I hear the echo of my own wondering thirst in his words. However unwanted it might be, I *do* desire Roane and I can tell that he returns the feeling. There's no point denying it to myself any longer, nor to him. He can see it in my body's response to his nearness, and if I'm reading desire in his avid gaze, then I'm sure he's reading it ten-fold in mine.

I've wanted this man ever since I first laid eyes on him, and there's no way he wouldn't be aware of it. Not when my glistening pussy is laid out directly in front of his eyes.

Does Nicole feel like this when Roane touches her? He says they don't have that kind of relationship, but how could they not, when this rope, like an extension of his hands, both contains and incites so much intense emotion? A flare of jealousy ignites deep in my belly, only adding to the mix of confusion and heady excitement.

"Yes," I start to answer. "This is…*oh*!" I gasp as one of his fingers slips inside my channel. I can't remember what I was about to say. I can only raise my mound upward, lifting my ass off the bench seat and using the ropes to help propel the lift. I push hard into his finger fuck, clenching my muscles around the digit and trying to force him deeper.

"Do you want to use your safe word, Ava?" He adds a second finger, thrusting as deep as he can, cupping my butt with his other hand and encouraging my back-and-forth rhythm. "You can. If you wish."

"No. I don't wish." I'm panting, speaking between clenched teeth, and that's when I hear the pattern of his breathing change and become almost as ragged as my own. I can't contain myself. A deep groan vibrates up and out of my throat. "*Roane*. I *hate* this. But I want you, so much."

I'm not sure what I'm asking, but as fast as he entered me, his fingers are gone from my body. I want him back inside me. I want him to release me from these shackles. I want to be fucked by him until I reach that delicious place of oblivion that a good orgasm brings. I want his hard cock rammed inside my body, buried right to the base so our bodies connect as one.

Oh God, I'm an emotional mess.

I drop my ass back onto the bench seat, hating the empty

feeling inside and somehow even more sensitized in that area than before he breached me with his fingers.

"All okay?" He checks my hands and feet, presumably for circulation problems, and I feel the moist slide of my own juices still fresh on his fingers as he touches me. I nod, wondering how he can move from pleasure to business and back again so effortlessly, when I'm craving him so badly I feel like I'm about to explode. I pray for him to return and give my greedy cunt more attention. I'm on fire, but definitely not with pain.

Instead he moves away, out of my line of vision. Where is he? What's he going to do next? Is he—?

"*Oh*!" He's working the pulley. With my arms strapped in front of my breasts and my torso wrapped in loops, I'm pulled inexorably upward off the bench. With one leg bent in half I'm off balance instantly and I have no choice but to let the rope take me. I expect him to stop when I'm fully standing but he keeps going past that limit until I'm forced onto the tiptoes of my unbound leg, and into a position where my body is tilted slightly backwards. My mound is even more exposed like this, with my bound leg pulled sideways. I have no proper purchase on the rug with my toes and no chance, even if I wanted it, to shield my pussy from his view.

Thank God I shaved everything this morning.

Now I *am* uncomfortable to the point of pain, but the protest that leaves my lips is still not my safe word. It sounds like a pathetic, inarticulate squeak. I'm not surprised it doesn't stop him. What's wrong with me? Why don't I just blurt out our agreed safety signal and be done with this nonsense?

When the lifting motion finally stops he reappears to stand in front of me. His eyes have darkened and his breathing is even shorter than it was. The further my immobi-

77

lization progresses, the more he is turned on. His lips are slightly parted and I see the glint of his teeth, and once again I'm reminded of a predatory tiger with its prey. His gaze is too strong, too intense and finally I can't take it any longer. I look away, twisting my head to the side.

Oh my God. "You're *naked*!" When did he remove his clothing? He's completely starkers, and he looks so fucking hot I almost orgasm on the spot. His erection is even more impressive than the constraints of his trousers hinted at, and I laugh a little to try and hide my ogling. My voice goes all squeaky, like it isn't working properly. "You have an all-over tan."

His skin cries out for my touch, and yet I can do nothing with these bound wrists but drink in the view. Soft and inviting, like rich creamy caramel, and yet the layers of hard muscle beneath are so clearly defined that he could easily work as a model, perhaps for a sexy aftershave campaign. I know from reading his bio that he's a couple of years older than me, but his physique is so finely honed he could pass for someone in his twenties.

Are we really going to do this in front of a crowd tomorrow night? I can't believe I'm here, hanging trussed up like the proverbial turkey, and all I can think about is *that* dick, the one right in front of me with its glistening tip decorated by a drop of pre-cum, forcing its way past the rope still lining my seam until its hard length is embedded deep inside me.

His head tilts as he studies me. "It's my natural skin tone."

"Oh. Lucky you. Most women would pay a fortune for—"

"Quiet, Ava." He lifts a hand, silencing my nervous babble. "I'm not going to keep you suspended. Not for your first time. But I want you to experience this before I lower you and complete my pattern work."

Just like that he leans over and takes one of my nipples into his mouth. He sucks it in, hard, and sensation explodes from that place of connection like fire through my veins. When he begins to suckle I squirm violently, my body desperate to release the responsiveness in some kind of action…or movement…*anything* that will allow me to let it all out. But I have to hang here, tethered, while the slip and slide of his lips on my breast creates exquisite torture and he flicks back and forth over the nipple with a clearly practiced tongue movement. The heat of that impressive cock sliding enticingly along my slit…

"*Yes*! Oh God, Roane, that feels so good!" He suckles even harder, taking a whole mouthful of breast as well as the nipple, almost as if he's trying to draw milk right out from the core of me, and a wonderful tugging starts deep down within my belly. Is that my womb, clenching and responding to his ministrations? My clit is so swollen it must look like a plump cherry, full and heavy between my legs. Is this what it's like to have balls, to have a cock? To have so much blood rushing to your sex that all you can do in the end is scream and let out the intense need?

My moan is rough, almost a growl. Roane answers against my breast with a responding groan that vibrates my flesh and enhances my desire. Finally he leaves that area, pressing light kisses over my rib cage and down across my stomach, skirting along and around the loops and knots with seemingly practiced ease. When he reaches my pussy I can no longer see him from this restrictive position, but his hot breath feathers across my sex and I know he's kneeling there in front of me, studying whatever engorged bits are currently on display. I'm wriggling like a worm on a hook as I anticipate his mouth, but when he slides the rope to one side and finally connects in that intimate kiss the reality is so much more than anything I could ever have anticipated.

His tongue parts my labia and circles my clit, so slick already with cream that he has no need to moisten it further. Then he is kissing and sucking in the most intimate place possible, as hard as he did on my breast, using his lips and tongue and even his teeth to scrape and suck and lick. He centers it all around the sensitized nub at my core, flicking fast with his tongue until the whole area is on fire.

"Yes, Roane, just there…" I'm falling…can't hang on… and I don't even notice the uncomfortable bite of these ropes anymore, I'm so desperate to climax. When he adds in a swiping movement up and down my slit with his thumb, then pushes up and into my channel again with his digit, it's finally too much. I can't hold on any longer and I burst right in his mouth with a screaming cry of release. He rides it with me, his mouth staying connected with my juicy cunt as I shudder and moan through my orgasm. Finally, eventually, I collapse, spent and exhausted and hanging like a limp rag.

He doesn't allow me time to recover. He rises up from the floor in a swift movement and leans over me, staring down. When he reaches around to grip my ass, my free leg automatically leaves the floor to wrap around his hips. His arms beneath my butt, and the rope suspension system, are now the only things holding me up. I have no choice but to trust him and relax, and when I finally bear down, giving him my full weight, he grunts and closes his eyes for a second.

"I never do this," he says.

What does he mean?

His eyes spring open and when they meet mine I see a hint of something new in their depths. *Vulnerability?* How can Roane be vulnerable? He's in control at all times; has to be for a session such as this to work. I don't understand, but I can't concentrate to try and figure it out because he's positioning the head of his cock at my channel entrance, and all I can think is how much I want this man. I want him so bad that right now nothing else matters.

"Please fuck me, Roane. Now."

He spreads my pussy and pushes until the tip of his cock is sucked into my channel. "I'm breaking my number one rule." He laughs briefly and the vibration shakes us both. "I don't even know why." He shoves up into my body, which is still spasming a little from my orgasm, and the thrusting movement hits that sweet spot deep inside. It sends me straight back over the edge. I scream and come again, only this time he's right there with me, plunging hard through the vaginal muscles contracting around him until he too, lets out a long shuddering moan and empties himself inside me.

We stay physically connected for what seems like hours, but I'm sure it's only a short space of time. Eventually he withdraws, a slight frown marring that perfect brow. I hope he unties me soon. Every part of my body aches and I'm not sure I'll even be capable of walking after this.

He's only gone for a few minutes and then he's back. I start to smile until I see he's holding something long and black in one hand. He's running the length of it almost lovingly through the fingers of his other hand. Not rope.

"Do you trust me, Ava?"

"What…" I'm still a little groggy from my double orgasm, and it takes a moment before I realize what it is. "No." I shake my head from side to side. "Not a flogger. I don't want—*ouch*!" He lashes out and catches me lightly across the hip. It's only a tiny sting, a taste of what might be in store if I agree to this.

"If you're going to heal fully you need to trust me."

Heal? "I…don't know if I can."

"You will need to trust in yourself, too. You have the strength, Ava. But it's your choice." He strokes the tails of the flogger across my breasts which are still sensitized from our coupling, and I almost moan at the delicate sensation. "Do I have your consent to do whatever it takes to help you find the freedom you crave?"

"I…" *Whatever it takes? How far will he go? Can I really trust him? Trust myself?* I close my eyes and offer a small nod. "Yes," I whisper, and then my eyes fly open as he places the flogger under my chin and lifts.

"Say it like you mean it. I won't do this without your permission."

I look deep into those green depths. His gaze is mesmerizing, but ultimately this is still my choice. *Freedom.* He's right. I *do* crave it. I nod again, this time more decisively. "Yes."

My reward is another sudden lash, and the shock of it reverberates right through me. I growl wordlessly, but he just shrugs and raises an eyebrow. ""If you want me to stop, use your safe word."

I narrow my eyes. "No." I will not show weakness. Not even after what we've just experienced.

A flicker of emotion crosses his face, but it's gone before I can read it. When he lashes me again, my voice shakes. "This isn't fun, Roane."

He gets close, right up in my face, and his voice is clear. "Then use. Your. Safe word." He punctuates his words with a light slap of the flogger and I can't stop the tears that well up in response.

"No." I won't give up, or give in. *Bastard.* This whole experience has gone from pleasure to humiliation in only a few short minutes and I can't keep up. I didn't expect this from him. I didn't expect it, for us.

"Are you angry with me, Ava?"

"No." *Yes, I'm fucking angry with you, Roane. And with*

myself for agreeing to this. I press my lips tightly together, not wanting to give him anything more. Not now. Not after *this*.

"*Liar*. Don't lie, Ava. Not to me. Not to *yourself.*"

On that last word he whips me again, twice in quick succession, and this time I can't contain the squeal.

"*Yes, I'm fucking angry!*" I hurl the admission in his direction, but it doesn't stop the barrage of stinging that follows. The thing that's been lurking through this whole experience, tucked safely deep down inside, lurches upward in response to the pain and all of a sudden I can't keep it tamped down anymore. Anxiety. Panic. Fear. Rage. It's all rising to the surface, and I can't stop it...can't control it, can't...

"*No!*" My body begins to shiver violently. I'm still balanced on one leg, completely at his mercy, and I can't stop this damn trembling that just gets worse and worse until I'm not holding myself up anymore, but being held completely by these flimsy little pieces of rope. I gasp, then a sob breaks free from my throat. I don't want to cry. I don't want to do this, I can't do this...and yet those fucking tears have already started dripping down my cheeks...

"I have you, Ava. Trust me. Let go. Let it out."

He drops the flogger, and my tears well up too fast to blink them back. *I can't do this. I can't.* A keening noise fills the room and I'm horrified when I realize it's coming from me. I turn my head and my reflection in that mirrored wall looks hideous. My mouth is wide-open and my eyes are streaming tears, and suddenly I'm shuddering and shaking and weeping like I've gone completely mad. "*Roane! What's happening?*" I scream out his name and he's there in a heartbeat. Gentle hands stroke my body, follow the curves, pause at my bindings before continuing in slow circular movements that soothe the pain and ground me.

"Cry, little one. Cry."

I do, with huge gulping sobs that I never knew would sound so loud once I finally let them out. I cry for Connor, my beautiful, damaged twin brother, who couldn't beat the drug habit that finally took his life, and I cry for the mother who may have protected us if she had survived beyond our birth. I cry for my failed relationship with my father, the man who put us through so much abuse, and all in the name of love. It was never physical bar the shouting, but always with the threat of violence hanging over us if Connor or I dared to be anything other than perfect. In the end I'm crying for me, for all the lost hopes and dreams of my childhood that got shut away into a tiny dark place in the back of my mind the day I discovered Connor high on pills and realized I had to take responsibility for his life as well as my own.

Most of all, I cry because Roane has reduced me to *this*. A snotty-nosed snivelling mess who can't even blow her own nose and clean herself up. I have no pride left. He has fucked me, and then stripped me bare. He has left me with nothing.

"Please," I sob, not even knowing what I'm asking for. "Please…"

A warm, moist cloth is on my face, wiping the tears and snot away, cleaning me up and giving me back a modicum of dignity.

"Good girl. I'm going to lower you now, Ava. You've done brilliantly." Roane's voice is tranquil in the oasis of emotion that still rocks my system, and in his words I finally identify something positive on which to focus.

Calm. He offers it, and finally I accept his offering. It descends, as smoothly as my physical descent from a state of hanging down toward the floor. Serenity trumps the panic as

Roane releases me from the rope pulley and finally I lay still and silent, and for the first time in...*ever*...I'm not consumed with fear. There is nothing I can do in this situation but accept. Nothing to do but relax into it...hand over responsibility...simply *be*...

My eyes close and I drift.

CHAPTER SIX

I'm not sure how long I lie here in this state. Eventually I realize he is checking my limbs again, running a fingernail across the back of my hands, and then doing the same on my feet. I frown at the sensation, and open my eyes to catch his satisfied nod.

"This is called subspace."

"Mmm." It's like I'm asleep, and yet I'm not. I'm definitely in a dream-like state where every movement, even my tiny nod, is slow. And yet somehow, every sensation is also heightened. I was hypnotized once, a few years ago, to try to combat my anxiety, and it feels something like that—aware of my surroundings but existing in a weightless, worry-free vacuum. *Heaven.*

The rug is warm and soft beneath me, its thick pile cushioning my body. "Connor told me about it. He loved this. Said it was the only thing other than pills that gave him peace." My voice is slurred. No wonder Connor loved being a sub. "I never really believed him. Till now." I've never felt such a sense of tranquillity.

I'm not really sure when Roane removes my bindings.

Coming back from the edge of wherever I've been occurs slowly, but then I realize he has freed me from all the rope and I'm lying in the fetal position, curled up on my side on the thick pile rug. Roane is lying there with me, his muscled body spooning mine and his arms forming a tight circle around me.

I'm safe. And yet I hurt. Every muscle in my body trembles with fatigue from the unfamiliar positioning during our session, and there are marks on my skin where the rope dug in and chafed. I'll have bruises all over by tomorrow. Rope burn at the very least. I regret nothing, though. I've never experienced such freedom, such release, as in this moment, when I've given over my whole self to his control.

He strokes my hair, then massages different parts of my body, encouraging the circulation to return to my extremities, and all the while he whispers encouraging words in my ear. He talks about how brave I am, and how strong, not because I withstood him but because I capitulated and let him in. "You're amazing, Ava. I know how impossible it is for you to let go. And yet you did."

His touch is delicate and I sense the loving care that he takes in soothing my limbs back to normality. An enormous sigh shakes my frame. "Thank you," I manage at last, and he gives me a gentle little squeeze before sitting up and turning so we're face to face. My body still doesn't work properly on its own, even though I continue to wriggle my fingers and toes every few seconds. Roane slides a finger beneath my chin to tilt my face up to his.

"It was my pleasure, Ava." There is genuine warmth in his gaze, a smile lifting his lips, and this close he looks older and more real. Perhaps for the very first time I see him as the man he is, rather than the stuff of myth and legend.

"Do you mean that?" I really am curious. How do I

compare to Nicole, his partner of several years? It must have been strange for Roane to do his thing with someone else. Trust. He forced it out of me, showed me what I'm capable of, until I gave it willingly. But doesn't trust work both ways? "I can't hide what you did for me. The effect you had on my body, Roane. What you did to release some of that...crap... inside me. But you... How... Was it..." I'm too afraid to finish my questions. What if he hated the last couple of hours and couldn't wait for it to be over? What if he's been laughing at my naiveté all this time, savoring the moment he can visit Nicole in hospital and share a joke about the wound-up stress-head executive who had her first orgasm in over a year then broke down into a blubbering mess?

My throat aches from trying to hold in the words and at first I'm mortified when my eyes begin to tear up. But then I think about what we've just experienced. Shedding a few tears is nothing, and it is definitely *not* a sign of weakness. If I've learnt one thing tonight, it is that. I go against instinct and let the tears well up and brim over, until there's a wet trail raining down my cheeks. I move until I'm lying again in his arms, resting the side of my face against his muscled chest and inhaling his delicious scent.

For answer he leans in and laps up my tears with the tip of his tongue. It tickles, and I can't help it. A light laugh escapes, followed by a hiccup.

"Oh, Ava," he says. Is that affection in his voice?

Our faces are so close I can see faint lines fanning out from the edges of his eyes, disappearing somewhere over those chiselled cheekbones. I can see that he hasn't shaved in several hours and he's developing a five o'clock shadow. It suits him, adding a rough edge to the otherwise controlled perfection of his face. I lift my arm experimentally. Yes, it's still working, despite the punishment my body has been through this evening. I touch his jawline, enjoying the rough texture beneath my fingertips.

When he leans down and kisses me I taste salt from my own tears coupled with an exotic flavor that is all Roane, and it's the sweetest thing I've ever tasted in my life. For a while I stop thinking anything at all. I just take his kiss, and give it back, our mouths dancing together in an experience that seems strangely more intimate than anything else we've done this evening. I'm not expecting the joy that fills my chest and when I gasp out loud he swallows the sound. Then he keeps kissing me, going deeper still. The connection is so intense as he plunges in with his tongue that it's as if we are truly making love with our mouths. This is completely unexpected, and wildly exhilarating, and I don't ever want it to stop.

His kiss is practiced and sure and yet there's something about it that also hints at uncertainty. Roane uncertain? It doesn't make sense. As soon as the thought crosses my mind he breaks off the kiss. His pupils are wide and his lips glisten with our combined moisture. He looks so incredibly sexy, at least until his brows come together in a frown.

What's the matter? "Did I do something wrong? Were we not supposed to...kiss?" I've never been in this situation before and maybe without realizing it, I broke a bondage rule.

He lets out an abrupt bark of laughter, but his eyes are not laughing anymore. They have closed over into pools of unreadable darkness. "Tiger," he says, into the growing silence, and my mouth drops open. He's using *my* safe word? Our safe word, I guess, but...

"I don't understand."

"Neither do I." He laughs again, briefly. "You're making me feel...hell, I don't know *what* I feel right this moment. Nicole and I...everything is straightforward. There's no sexual chemistry between us, it is purely professional. *Shibari*. What we just did, Ava…"

"Didn't we just do shibari too?"

"In essence, yes. But it was far more than that. It was what I call *kinbaku*. An emotional exchange as much as a sexual one. It happens very rarely for me and I was not prepared. I *never* get emotionally involved with my models. And yet with you…it confuses me. *You* confuse me. Our roles are less clearly defined than they should be."

While he's talking he helps me sit up properly, and when he pauses I use the bench seat as a final crutch to stagger to my feet. "Can someone be submissive and dominant at the same time?" I'm still trying to understand what happened here today. It's going to take a long time for it all to sink in.

"Yes, Ava. There is a term that I believe may apply to you. Alpha submissive. You are like me. Dominant in most aspects of your life. But there is a need deep inside you that will never be satisfied unless you give in and allow yourself to submit every now and again."

He's right. I sense it stirring, like a tangible thing, and it craves so much more from Roane than what he's already provided.

"It intrigues me, Ava. *You* intrigue me. I've never met anyone quite like you."

This, coming from *him*? "I'm just an ordinary woman, Roane."

"You are far from ordinary, my love. You are quite possibly the strongest—and at the same time perhaps also the most vulnerable—person I've ever met. As a consequence I'm not letting you into that shibari theatre tomorrow night. It would destroy you."

Now we face the real "tiger" in the room. He's right, of course. I can't *bear* the thought of exposing myself like this in front of even one other person. But who else is going to step up and do it? "Roane, the festival has to succeed, and to do that we need to—"

"No."

"I owe it to my brother—"

"No."

His mouth is set in a straight, stubborn line. I can see this needs some negotiation. "Why not? That's what tonight was about, wasn't it? To see if we could do this together."

"That was before."

"Before what?"

"Before tonight. You're not doing this again, *ever*, except in private, with *me*."

"But—"

"It will destroy you," he says again. "You're so vulnerable and you've had too much hurt in your life. I'm going to protect you from now on."

"Wait." I hold up a hand, not able to process it. "You... want to protect *me*?" No one's ever offered to do that. Not once in my whole life. *I'm* the protector. Always have been.

"Of course. I will find someone else for the show."

"You said there wasn't anyone else available."

"Trust me, Ava. I will find someone. And besides..." He gestures downward and my eyes widen when I encounter his virile erection, so strong it's almost vertical. When did that start up again? He really does have the most magnificent penis. "I'm the Master. I cannot allow my audience to see that I don't always have full control over my body."

My legs are suddenly not working too well and I sit back down on the bench. But my grin is wide and hopefully inviting as I pat the bench seat next to me. "Don't you? Why *is* that, I wonder?"

He accepts my invitation and sits, leaning back to rest his

arms along the top of the bench backing. "You know damn well why, beautiful Ava."

For answer I do what I've been dying to do since the moment I saw him on that shibari stage in New York. I lean down and take his cock deep into my mouth and throat, sucking in all that gorgeous flavor and finally staking my claim. *You're mine, Roane.*

My reward is a throaty growl, and words that whisper above my head and make my heart swell with anticipation for the future. "Ava, my submissive. My alpha. *Mine.*"

The End

I hope you enjoyed ALPHA SUBMISSIVE. Want more in the FORBIDDEN series? Keep reading for WATCH ME.

WATCH ME

A VOYEURISM ROMANCE

PREFACE

Isabel and her sexy neighbor play an erotic game of voyeurism, but when Izzy's husband Will discovers her Sunday night secret the tables turn and the watcher suddenly becomes the watched.

"I was so afraid, when my husband uncovered my dirty little secret. Afraid that he'd hate me, or think me disgusting, or somehow be completely turned off. Equally scared that this watching game I play with our sexy neighbor might be shut down for good. Can Will bring himself to join our addictive Sunday night ritual, or will I be forced into an impossible choice between the man I love, and the sexual urges that consume me?" ~ *Isabel*

CHAPTER 1

ISABEL

My hands clutch like claws against the window pane. The glass, frosted by Melbourne's mid-winter cold, is icy beneath my fingertips. I let the coolness seep into my flesh, grounding me. I am waiting, but he's late.

We have an arrangement, this neighbor of mine and me. At the start of every working week, late on a Sunday night while the rest of the city sleeps, we play a game. A dangerous, addictive game.

I don't even know his real name, and yet this game of ours, and his presence in my life, has grown to fill the recent emptiness. It consumes me. *He* consumes me, but in a good way. I am becoming whole again, thanks to this man and our seductive, secret play.

But it is half past midnight and he is not yet at his post. The window in the apartment across the narrow alleyway is still dark. The red brickwork surround is lit by a street lamp that only serves to enhance the darkness within, making the square appear fathomless. It looks like an empty eyeball socket in a skull whose soul has long departed the physical world.

A thought grips my heart and squeezes painfully. Perhaps he's grown tired of it all? Perhaps he no longer wishes to play?

A whimper slips from my lips and the resultant breath frosts the glass in front of my face, obscuring my reflection. What will I do to satisfy this insatiable need if he's not here anymore to fill the void? My shoulders slump and even though I'm reluctant to give up this lonely vigil, I am about to concede when a square of golden warmth lights the window opposite. Just like that, between one click of a switch and the next, my anxiety turns to heady excitement.

Yes! I need this. I need you.

A tremble runs through my limbs and centers between my thighs, igniting an ache of pleasure. The folds of flesh housing my clit are already slick with anticipation, but the jolt from his appearance causes additional cream to anoint my labia lips. When I shift, they slide against one another in a slippery reminder of how much he turns me on. He can do that, just by strolling across his bedroom toward the ensuite in the next room, casually shucking off his black T-shirt as he passes the floor-to-ceiling window.

There is a fluidity to his movement that speaks of self-assurance. I wish I had his confidence. I wish I had his "devil-may-care" attitude. He seems to have that rare and incredibly seductive quality most of us crave and never quite achieve— the ability to *know* his own body and to be comfortable in his own skin.

My neighbor is, quite honestly, the most beautiful man I've ever seen. Not Hollywood-perfect by any means, but handsome in a rugged, hard-edged way that screams power and exudes sensuality.

I still love my husband despite recent events, but William is an ordinary man. He wouldn't mind me saying that. I'm the same. Will turned forty only a few weeks ago and I'm heading faster than I'd like toward that age, too. There's nothing particularly special about either of us, but the same cannot be said for this neighbor of ours.

He is different. I have never known anyone like him. Never seen anyone like him. Never *watched* anyone like him.

I'm guessing he's in his early thirties—that perfect age when a man's looks have matured into strength and authority, but they are not yet to the point where his still-youthful appearance has started to dissipate.

His hair is a dark chocolate brown, slightly too long, and a little messy around the edges. It's the kind of hair that screams out for a woman to run her fingers through the disobedient locks in an attempt to tame them, when she knows all the while that the effort will probably be futile. No part of this man is meant to be tamed, not even that gorgeous hair.

I think his eyes are blue. Though the back alley that separates each of our respective buildings is only a few meters wide, he rarely looks this way and it's hard to confirm whether I'm correct. I imagine a color unlike any blue I've ever seen. A shade as clear as a spring sky—light aqua—and offering a decadent yet much-needed promise of the satisfaction to come for anyone who visits his abode.

Oh, God. Just the thought of those eyes darkening in pleasure as they catch a glimpse of my naked flesh sends another delicious shiver across my skin and a super-charged pulse to my core.

I move closer to the glass, rubbing my breasts back and forth against its cold surface and pretending he's rubbing an ice cube over the sensitive tips. It's one advantage of winter, that freezing glass; the shock of it against my taut nipples only adds to the heat between my legs.

I send him a silent message before stepping back into the shadows.

I want to feel your mouth on these breasts. Sucking. Licking. Leaving bite marks on my swollen, aching flesh.

His body is long and lean and he moves like a caged wild cat, prowling across his bedroom with barely contained impatience. Yet he's graceful in his movements, too. Watching him move is like watching a ballet, only this ballet is usually X-rated, filled with sexual vignettes that titillate and tease the audience into a zone of shuddering orgasmic pleasure.

Yep. I'm nearly there already tonight, and we haven't even begun.

If I were wearing underwear right now it might contain the moisture signalling the extent of my desire, but I'm not. On Sundays, after midnight, I wear nothing but my red stilettos, and the diamond pendant earrings my mirage lover left in the mail box a few weeks ago.

There was no note with the earrings, but I know it was *him*. My husband doesn't buy jewellery as he says it's a waste of hard-earned money. Will would far rather put our spare cash into a retirement plan for the future. But it's more than the extravagance of the gift that signalled the giver. I know it was my neighbor across the alleyway who provided the delicate drops because the package was addressed to "*The exotic beauty in the red high heels,*" and Sunday night is the only time I ever wear these shoes.

He called me exotic. *Me*? No one has *ever* called me that. I'm not slim the way I used to be twenty years ago. I'm nowhere near being a beauty, either. Never have been. But the joy that filled me at his words decorated my lips for days, and I made sure to wear the earrings the next time we played.

That was the night he broke the rules and looked across, just for a moment, actually acknowledging my presence.

When he squeezed lightly at his ear lobe the gesture sent a clear message. He was pleased I'd worn his gift. The lopsided grin that accompanied the gesture transformed his somewhat severe features and an answering smile trembled on my lips. Then he sauntered away, but my smile remained.

I've worn his gift every week since, and now I have a pet name for the man who consumes my fantasies. Diamond Dan. Danny. My elusive, untouchable lover.

Tonight my thoughts scream to Danny, desperate to communicate how much he's come to mean in my life and my heart. My throat aches with wanting but, as always, my voice must remain silent.

Finally you are here. You'd better be ready to play, you naughty boy.

CHAPTER 2

I fist one of my hands and bang the glass, just the once. I want to let him know his tardiness is noted, and I see his lips quirk as he receives and understands my message.

Yes, we are close enough to read the subtle nuances in each other's expressions. Close enough to hear the sounds of sex, if we choose to open our windows, though tonight it's far too cold for that. We are even close enough for the scent of sex, if we choose to inhale. And I have done that, in the past. He smells incredible when he's fully turned on.

We are close enough for almost everything. Except taste, of course, and touch.

Dan and I will never touch in this game of ours. Just as children are advised to do when they enter a shop that holds items of value, so we too, as adults, have chosen to look but not touch, lest we devalue what the other has to offer.

My breath hitches when I realize he has a friend with him this evening. A woman has followed him into the room. My lips curve upward and with an effort I try to resume breathing evenly.

Inhale. Exhale. A woman! Oh Danny, you know that's my favorite.

Watching him with another woman makes it so much easier to imagine those long-fingered, capable hands caressing my own body.

I can't get enough of watching him with another woman... The way he grips the back of her head so firmly when he draws her close to kiss her parted lips. The way his fingers disappear somewhere beneath the thick waves of her hair—a chestnut color tonight and only slightly lighter than my own.

I love the way he sucks on her bottom lip first, nibbling gently as if sampling her flavor before committing properly to the kiss.

Yes. Kiss her like that, until the flare of passion becomes fully ignited and you suddenly slam your groin into hers. Force her legs apart with one of your powerfully muscled thighs so she can ride you hard and that kiss becomes deeper and less controlled.

I'm starting to pant as I touch myself between the legs, my fingers circling my bud and teasing it out from between the folds now engorged with the heat of desire. But it isn't enough. He's grinding against her and she's doing the same back to him. There's nothing between them but a few pieces of clothing and soon those impediments will be ripped away, too.

I want that feeling of hard grind. I *need* it. I miss it.

Making love with Will used to induce that mood; the one where we were both balanced on the knife-edge of control and it felt like anything could happen. He and I were always good together in bed. I *love* that defining moment during sex, when the balance shifts and you fall headlong into a state where thought ceases and mindless madness reigns. Yes, we had that, Will and I, often, until...

Stop! Don't think about it. Concentrate instead on Danny and the woman he's chosen to pleasure this evening.

My hand shifts until I'm cupping my mound. I smack the flesh, jumping a little at the sting when I go a bit overboard on the pressure. It feels so satisfying I do it again, over and over, slapping hard until pain mixes effortlessly with the pleasure and I can't bear the thought of continuing. But I don't want to stop, either. *It feels so fucking good.*

Harder. Stop. Faster. Stop. *I don't want to come yet. It's way too soon.*

They are both shucking off the rest of their clothing with a frenzied edge that has their hands shaking and their mouths parting and then returning as if eager for more.

What does he taste like, during their kiss? Does he finish his meals with coffee, or perhaps a liqueur of some kind, leaving his breath rich and malty with layers of complex flavor? Is he a smoker? Or is he mint-fresh and clean, like a refreshing breeze on a mid-summer's day?

I lick my lips to moisten them, imagining how it would feel to suck in his breath, take his tongue deep, and offer mine in return.

Finally they're naked and his hands knead her generous butt cheeks, working the rounded white flesh with a desperation that will probably leave her with bruises. I'm sure she doesn't care, though. Especially when he pulls her in like that, impossibly close against his fit, muscled form. How could any woman worry about a bruise or two when she's being held in such a strong embrace?

It must feel like heaven to be encased in Danny's arms. I cup my belly, imagining the hot, hard feel of his cock pressed just *there*. Is his organ leaking pre-cum across her stomach even now, until their bodies begin to slip and slide in a damp, sensual dance? Or is it instead thrusting along her seam, using her labia lips as a makeshift channel until he can finally drive up and inside the real thing?

I rock back and forth against the window frame, imitating their movement and wishing the firm edge of the sill was Danny getting ready to fuck *me*.

My pussy is greedy. It wants to suck him in and hold him with tight muscles until neither of us can take anymore and I explode around him in out-of-control, clutching spasms. A tiny whimper escapes my lips and I stagger back from the window ledge. *Too much. Not yet.*

Dan lifts her suddenly, his arm muscles flexing as he takes her weight, and she wraps her legs tight around his hips. Beneath her ass, the shadow of his balls teases my vision in a gentle bounce as he carries her across to the bed and dumps her right in the middle of the king-sized mattress.

"Ooh, that's a bit rough," I chastise him quietly, watching his companion rebound a little before steadying herself. But she seems to like it that way. Her knees bend up and her legs drop wide, one to each side, opening her cunt to his—and my —view. Gorgeous and wet, like a dark pink flower opening to the sun, and at its center is a pearl all ready for his tasting.

Danny climbs onto the bed and kneels above her, staring down. His shoulders are wide and his hips are narrow. It's a perfect body curve that just cries out to be explored with eager fingers. He must work out at a gym to get such a tightly-honed physique.

He twists for a moment toward the window, almost as if he's allowing me a better view of his cock. I was right. It *is* jutting out and up, and even at this distance I can see the glistening tip. He's leaking with pre-cum, so much so that when he takes his own organ in hand and begins stroking up and down I can almost hear the delicious squelching sound.

I love watching him eat out his female companions, and I let out a shuddering sigh when he finally obliges and turns back to the task. I can't see his organ any longer, but the flex of those tight muscles in his buttocks as he leans over her offers additional visual fodder and feeds the pang of excitement flooding my body.

There's just something so sensual about the way he parts her folds to find the central nub. The way he uses one long finger to stroke gently up her slit, all the way from the back of her ass to the front, then lingering there, around her clit. The way he holds her flaps open as if studying her, then finally settles in more deeply between her legs, dipping in with what seems to be only the very tip of his tongue. Touching, tasting, and feathering her sensitive place in such a delightfully delicate manner.

Yes, Dan. Sink your face into her muff and suck the juices from her core. Taste how much she wants you. Lick her clit until it shines like a ripe cherry, then pluck it. Eat it. Enjoy her flavor, and then prepare her for more.

CHAPTER 3

S he's moaning now. I can't hear it with our windows closed against the cold, but I can see the grimace of pleasure on her face as her mouth drops open and her eyes screw shut and I *know* that keening sound wrenching from her throat. It's the same one forcing its way past *my* lips.

Danny's face is hidden deep between her thighs as he pleasures her, the ripple of muscle in his upper arms and legs apparent as he rocks gently back and forth.

My clit swells at the carnal tableau and I'm so full of desire I can't stand still. I lean forward, resting the side of my face flush against the glass, enjoying the bite of cold on my hot cheek. I clutch briefly at the firm wooden frame to maintain balance as the blood rushes from every part of me to the very center of my need.

My pelvis thrusts a little of its own accord. I'm humping the air and it isn't enough. I want to be fucked. Or maybe I want to fuck. Maybe I want both. The hunger grows until I can't take it anymore.

Not enough. I have to touch. I pinch the erect tips of my swollen breasts with fingers that are so unsteady the prizes slip out of my grip. Frustrated, I change tactics and feather back and forth across my nipples, enjoying their hard pebble feel against the soft cushion of my palms. Sensation explodes outward, like a satisfying wave that goes on and on.

Oh God! These exquisite visual displays that Danny provides every week are as addictive as a drug, and I'm like an addict who just can't get enough.

If his mouth were between *my* legs right now, he'd be licking and sucking *there*, right in the spot where one of my hands has finally traversed downward from my breast. He'd suck hard, willing my clit into a mini-erection of its own, pulling it out from its hooded sheath until shudders wrack my whole body and I can hardly stand up.

You eat pussy so well, Danny. Better than anyone else I've ever observed.

As if responding to my thoughts, he lifts his head and glances around. His mouth is slightly swollen and slick from her body fluids. His tongue darts out in a little pink flash, clearly enjoying a final taste before he straightens up and turns to display the full beauty of his rigid cock to my eager gaze.

I adore Danny's cock. It is large without being scary-big, and when it's hard it rises up almost vertically, proclaiming his virile male strength like nothing else can.

Pressure builds in all the right places in my body, and my chest lifts and falls unevenly as my breathing quickens. I'm close to coming, and so is he. That determined look on his face, edged with desperation, tells me he's very near.

He readies himself to enter her and I strain to capture the moment he plunges deep. *Yes*! He shoves hard, both of them clearly so wet the entry plays out like an easy glide. He thrusts again, seating himself more firmly inside and her legs rise up to clasp his waist and hold him there.

She's wearing black nail polish on her toes. I've only just noticed it, and as he pumps back and forth inside her I watch those dark-tipped toes of hers shake and shudder in the air. Little droplets of black in a blazing golden tableau.

Her arms are spread-eagled, one to each side, and he has her wrists imprisoned in a vice-like grip. Her head is turned toward me, her mouth open in what looks like a howl. I stop thrusting against my own hand and stand super-still, straining to listen.

Yes. I think I hear her. It's a faint wail that sounds a little bit like a cat in pain. It could equally be a woman in the throes of ecstasy and I choose to believe the latter. It's her, for sure. When her eyes roll up in her head and her features suddenly squeeze tight I know she's nearly at the end.

And so am I. My reflection in the window is like a mirror image of what I'm seeing across the alley, though my eyes are open, not scrunched. My face sports the same wide-mouthed, slack-jawed expression as hers, and the sounds from my throat have become guttural, almost choked.

Are these the sounds she's making right now?

I bend lower so I can slide a finger up inside my channel. Not nearly as satisfying as Danny's gorgeous cock, but imagine if it were…

I search for that sweet spot inside, the one I only discovered recently when I bought my first dildo from an internet sex toy store. Who knew that the pleasure of a clit orgasm could be ramped up a hundred-fold if you add internal stimulation to the mix? I certainly didn't, until I tried it out for myself with a fake vibrating penis that looks just about the same size as Danny's.

Both of my hands are now working my sex. One inside, one out. Double the pleasure.

Danny. Fuck her. Fuck me. Make us both scream when

we come.

I want to catch a glimpse of his face but can't quite see it from this angle. I know from past experience that he'll have a mask-like expression; a rictus of concentration and focus. A bright sheen of sweat appears on his back, accentuating the tone of his muscles more effectively than a jar of oil ever would. This is *real*. This is so fucking *hot*.

And then I catch it; the instant he loses control and the frenzy begins. I moan, plunging as deep as I can into my own body as I try to keep up the pace. He's lost the even rhythm and he's riding her so hard the top of her skull keeps whacking the headboard.

Then even through the closed windows I hear the high-pitched scream as she starts to come. His whole body begins to shudder as I watch him follow her over the edge.

"Yes! Yes! Oh my *God*..." The squeal forces all the way up from the base of my lungs and bursts out into our bedroom as I buck crazily against my hands. Dampness is smeared across my palms and I lose all sense of time. The orgasm takes me to a place where everything stands still and nothing exists but these waves of sensation that keep rolling and rolling through every part of my body.

Finally, eventually, I come back to the present. I sigh deeply, replete and exhausted, until a guttural masculine groan to my right causes my heart to jolt painfully.

I gasp, having forgotten that Danny and I are not the only players in this sensual game of voyeurism.

I swivel just in time to catch the creamy arc of cum spurt up and out, and then down, the spray eventually losing itself in the cream-colored carpet of our bedroom.

Will. My husband. He's been there in the shadows, taking his own private pleasure. Watching the watcher. Watching *me*.

CHAPTER 4

WILLIAM

I *love* watching Izzy like this. I don't know if she'll ever realize just how much I love it. The debauched sounds that come out of her mouth. The involuntary arching of her back when she's in the throes of passion. The clenching of every muscle in her body just before she comes. The way her cunt gives away the extent of her pleasure when it releases shiny liquid along her seam before dripping down her inner thighs. The euphoric expression on her face as she watches that bastard across the street...

Those sounds, and that look on her face, are why I sit here in the corner chair whenever I can get away early from work. So I can observe her at an angle and fully enjoy the priceless rapture that transforms her from my ordinary, everyday wife into a wanton, sex-crazed siren.

That look is what now fuels my every waking fantasy and guides my fist in pumping harder and faster around my dick every chance I can get.

I want to make her forget *him*, and come back to me. *I* want to be able to give her that ecstatic look once again. I used to, before the blip in our marriage. Well, yeah, okay.

More than a blip. I slept with someone else. Once. And a mutual friend made sure Izzy found out.

I've been trying so hard since then to make it up to her. I *love* Isabel. She's my world. We met at high school when I was sixteen and she was almost fifteen. Back then a year made all the difference and I was the sexy "older man". The way she used to look up to me was such a fucking turn-on.

She's the first woman I ever loved. The *only* woman I've ever been with sexually, apart from that one night at the conference in Sydney eighteen months ago, when I had way too much to drink.

What was I thinking that night? Fuck knows. Maybe I finally wanted to see what it felt like to be with another woman. Maybe the other guys egged me on, making me feel like a failure for only having ever been with the one partner. Maybe I was just another drunk, stupid dick who got caught up in the moment and didn't think about consequences until afterward.

Consequences. Yeah. Not thinking at all, I guess, and when I realized how much I'd hurt Isabel...

We've been working through it all with a marriage counsellor since then. Trying to claw things back, but it hasn't been the same. The trust is gone and I'm going to have to earn it back. One day. If I can.

I think that's partly why it was such a shock when I came home early from my shift that night just over a month ago, and discovered her sprawled against the window in our darkened bedroom, panting and close to orgasm as she watched our neighbor across the back alleyway drill hard and fast between another man's tight little ass cheeks.

I hadn't seen that sex-hazed look on her face in *so long*...

"What the *fuck*, Izzy? Two guys?"

I remember how fast her head swivelled toward me, a

suddenly stricken expression shifting her features from ecstasy to horror, and her hand lifting up from her shaved pussy—when the hell had she shaved it?—to cover her open mouth.

"*Will*! I didn't expect you home for another hour or two."

Clearly. I shook my head from side to side, trying to clear the shock. Izzy looked hotter than I'd ever seen her, even with embarrassment coloring her cheeks, and my body instantly betrayed me when the blood rushed south to ignite a heavy ache in my groin.

"Yeah, well." My voice came out gruff and I cleared my throat. "Thought I told you the restaurant will be closed tomorrow so we can get ready for the foodie event that's rolling out across Melbourne. They let the kitchen staff finish early tonight." I'm a sous chef and I don't normally get home from work till late, but the upcoming annual food festival was a big deal, and the first time our restaurant had been approached to participate.

"Oh, sure. I...forgot."

Her voice was breathy and sexy-as-hell, and I had no idea why we were still talking normally when she was standing there stark naked. Well, except for those teetering red heels that made her legs look longer and more luscious than usual. When did she buy those? I immediately pictured her hooking those long legs up over my shoulders as I plunged deep inside her body, and my perfectly serviceable work trousers were suddenly way too tight.

Izzy's brown hair was loose down her back in a sea of waves, her lips slightly parted, and her hazel eyes were still half-closed with the remnants of whatever had just been going on. Unlike the room across the road, which had a floor-to-ceiling window lit up like Christmas, our room was mostly dark. But there was a streetlamp in the alley outside that threw a golden hue across her bare skin, creating mysterious shadows and highlighting curves in a way that gave her body an unusually sensual edge.

She looked different that night, in front of the window. Younger. More...wanton. She looked fucking incredible, actually. With the backdrop of those two guys going at it hard and fast behind Izzy's darkened silhouette, the heaviness in my cock intensified, and I had a full-on erection in record time.

"Jesus, Isabel." I shifted, trying to accommodate the hard-on, but the rasp of trouser fabric on my flesh only made the swelling worse. "I haven't seen you look that hot in...*fuck*! You like to *watch*? Why didn't I know this about you? I'm your husband, for Christ's sake."

CHAPTER 5

She looked like she was about to burst into tears. I remember how she stumbled away from the window, fumbling with the cord of the blinds. Should I go comfort her? She was clearly distraught and I let go of the door handle and moved further into the room, not sure what to say or do. I stepped closer but she wrapped her arms around her middle, hugging herself, and the pose seemed to scream, "Back off".

I paused, my heart already pounding so hard the beat echoed way up in my throat, and I had so many random thoughts running through my head that I couldn't find a coherent thread.

I want to fuck her right now. How could she do this? It's my fault; I must have driven her to it. Watching? She likes to watch? Oh my God, she looks so fucking hot...

"I'm really sorry, Will. I—"

"How long has this been going on?"

"Um." She took a deep breath and it came out kind of wobbly. Fragile-sounding. "About...four months."

"So..." I tried to calculate, but my head was still fuzzy

with shock. "Must have been..." I frowned. "Just after he moved in, then?"

She nodded. The movement swished her hair and I realized it had gotten long in the past year or so. It suited her long. "Yes. It was an accident, the first time. It was late, and you were at work, as usual." She shrugged. "I was on my way to bed, walking past our bedroom window and I realized he was...you know...*masturbating*, without having closed his curtains."

She stumbled over the word and I almost laughed. She couldn't say masturbate without blushing, and yet she could stand in front of an uncurtained window and do it herself. While watching a complete stranger go at it, too. Before I could say anything more, she continued. "The light was on over there, so it was really easy to...see."

The light was on? *Right.* What sort of guy jacks off in front of a lighted open window when he's just moved in to a brand-new neighborhood? I hated him from that moment on.

But when I shot a glance across to the neighbor in question, just in time to see the shudder of release as he presumably emptied himself inside the guy's ass, and the creamy squirt of cum shooting over the bed from the other guy on all fours, my own hard-on twitched and I had to fight the urge to reach down and start pumping right then and there.

No wonder Izzy was fascinated. The view from here was so clear it was almost like being in the room with them. I had to admit, the guy was pretty fit-looking, and now that he'd withdrawn from his partner's ass and disposed of the condom I could see the full extent of his well-endowed assets.

Fucking bastard. I've never looked like that, not even fifteen or twenty years ago when I was still relatively young.

"So, you like watching...*guys* have sex?" I couldn't get

my head around it, but she let out a nervous-sounding chuckle and shook her head.

"He's not gay. He seems to like, well, all kinds of people. Men *and* women."

My eyebrows rose. "At the same time?"

"No. Well, not always."

"Not..." I cleared my throat, and a bark of laughter finally slipped out before I could stop it. *My wife's been getting off to group stuff?*

What the hell had been going on here right under my ignorant nose? The lounge chair in the corner of our room suddenly looked real comfortable and I sank down onto it before my unsteady legs gave way.

"Does he know you're...you know. *Watching*? If he doesn't..." *It's illegal.* I didn't want to voice the last part of that sentence out loud, but the relief that swept through me when Izzy nodded turned my bones to mush. Lucky I was already sitting down.

"Yes. He doesn't usually engage or anything, but...yes. Even that first time. It was kind of like he did it on purpose right in front of the window, looking for someone who would take the bait and...watch."

And it was *my wife* who took the bait. My lips tightened, but then her shoulders lifted in a small shrug as she continued. "He always tells his partners before they start, too. I see their startled glance over here, but mostly they seem okay with it. He always shuts the curtains if they're not. I think..." She hesitated, then blurted out, "I'm pretty sure they *like* knowing I'm here."

Her tears came then, silently. They just welled up in those sad eyes, adding a green luminosity to the hazel, before brimming over and dropping down her cheeks.

"*Don't*, Izzy." I hate it when she cries. Especially lately, when I feel like everything is somehow my fault.

"I'll stop, Will. I promise—"

"*No.*" I sucked in a breath and let it out slowly, trying to release my resentment over that bastard drawing *my* Izzy into such a crazy game.

After a moment I was back in control, and I held out my hands and beckoned her over. When she was standing in front of me her erect nipples were right at my eye height, and I wanted nothing more than to lean forward and suck them in, working her into a frenzy the way I used to.

Remember what sex was like with me, *Isabel? I can give you that dazed expression again. If you'll just let me back in.*

Instead I lifted one of her hands to my mouth so I could graze my lips gently across her palm. "Please don't cry, and don't..." I swallowed hard, wondering if I could do this. She seemed to need it, and after what I did to our marriage I sure didn't have any right to say no to her needs. "Don't stop." *There. See. It was easy.* "Go back to the window and do... whatever it is you do when I'm not here. I want to see it."

She was already shaking her head. "No Will, I can't possibly—"

"Yes, you *can.*" I let go of her hands and reached down to undo the top button of my trousers. "Do it, Izzy. Trust me. I'm not turned off by this."

I might have still been furious at that fucking exhibitionist bastard across the street, but that didn't change how I felt about Isabel. If *this* is what it took to turn her on, then I'd be right there on the ride with her.

She must have seen the truth of my words in the hard flesh that sprang free when I released the zipper. A timid smile broke through her tears, turning her features radiant and wiping away the sadness. "Are you sure?"

"Izzy. You've practically creamed that window ledge already. I can see it still glistening all over your legs. *Trust* me when I say I want to watch." My voice had gone all gruff. *Surely to God she can gauge how turned on I am?*

She laughed and hiccupped at the same time. "I do still love you, Will. You know that, don't you?"

I nodded, shifting in the chair to a more comfortable position and taking my cock in hand. "Yeah." *God, I'm ready to explode. I'll probably hit the roof for once, and have cum dripping back down on our heads.*

"I *need* this. I never realized it before Danny came along, but I do."

Danny? She knew the bastard's name? "I can see that, hon, that's why…" I shrugged. Words didn't seem enough, but I said it anyway. "I love you too, Izzy. I just want you to be happy again." My voice broke on those last words, but I remember that first night it was as if I hadn't spoken at all. She'd already turned back toward the window.

"He was late tonight." Will's voice from the darkness is low, a thread of both irritation and sated desire running through it. He's not one for patience; never has been. "But I guess he must've come through in the end. *Jeez*, that was good, Izzy. You looked so fucking gorgeous when you came. You always do."

He shifts in the chair, leaning his head against the back, and the springs protest. If we keep this up every week we'll probably need to replace that chair before too long. All that pelvis thrusting from Will is wearing out the support.

He prefers to leave his clothes on while he watches, letting his organ jut free from the zipper opening of his trousers, and fisting the turgid flesh when things get heated. He says the rasp of the fabric against his skin is a turn-on, as if he's out in public and indulging himself under the dubious cover of a linen-covered restaurant table.

I prefer the freedom of nudity. It's like everything is pared back to the basics, and I can concentrate on watching without the fetters of society dictating what I should or shouldn't feel.

"Thanks, hon. Glad I could oblige." I flash him a quick

grin. I'm in that happy, post-orgasmic state where my usual embarrassment has disappeared, and his answering chuckle tells me we'll both sleep well tonight.

The watcher, and the watched. A double edge to this game that's been unexpectedly enjoyable.

Will walked in on me about a month ago while I was watching Danny take his pleasure. That particular time it was with a male friend, though it could have been either. Danny is so popular, his allure so seductive, that it doesn't surprise me when he attracts both men and women to his boudoir.

The intriguing question is *why*. Why so many, and why so often? Is he going for the Olympic record of lovers? Is it because the people he invites back to his home decide not to return for a second visit, or is it Danny himself who doesn't want to engage with them more than once? Is he commitment-phobic? The possibilities in his story fascinate me, but I can't quite work him out.

If he were to invite me over there, into his bedroom, I think I would fight harder than I've ever fought for anything to stay there. I'd *never* want to leave.

Sometimes, in those dark moments that arrive unexpectedly—usually in the middle of the night when I'm worrying about Will's and my future—I ponder our arrangement. Am I somehow, "the one?" Am I the only constant in Dan's love life? I'm here every week, waiting pressed against the window, and yet strangely, so is he, whether accompanied or on his own. In a bizarre way, I feel that I've come to be as important to Danny as he is to me. Of *course* he knows I'm here. And yet, no matter who he brings home, male or female, I'm here in the shadows, and the idea that he enjoys my subtle presence fills me with a sense of purpose.

He needs me.

He always talks to his partner right before they start, and I can pinpoint by their stunned glance in my direction the moment he reveals they have an audience. I've been really surprised at how many of them don't actually mind. I never knew so many people like the idea of being watched.

Usually there's an instant of shock. A few seconds of resistance in which I observe the push and pull of both fascination and revulsion reflected in their features. I *love* that moment. A bubble of laughter fills my chest and I hold my breath to see which way the night will play out. Usually the titillation takes over and their resistance melts away to nothing, until we all end up together in this crazy game.

Only once since this started has my mirage lover shrugged in apparent regret before leaning across to close his blinds and block me out. The woman he was with that time stood scowling and holding her arms tight across her midriff, until the golden picture winked out of existence behind those heavy curtains. That night he looked directly at me for several seconds, the longest he's ever held my gaze, and I'm sure I saw regret softening his features. He touched his fingertips to his lips for a moment, then pressed them to the window pane right before he drew the curtains, and I looked at those smudges on the glass until even the thin edge of light around his curtains was extinguished and nothing was visible but darkness.

I cried myself to sleep that night, with silent gulping breaths, pretending to be asleep when Will finally came home from work, and trying hard not to wake him as my tears made wet tracks from the corners of my eyes down into my hair.

It was the very next day that my diamond earrings appeared in our mail box.

He thinks I'm beautiful. When I wear them, I *feel* beautiful. The thought makes me want to dance around the room, but Will would probably think I was crazy. Instead I stand still, watching. And waiting.

"Is he done, over there?"

Will's voice brings me back to the present and I glance toward Dan's bedroom to see the light on in the ensuite bathroom. We know his routine by now. When he's had enough for the night, he usually ushers his companion—or companions—out the door almost immediately and heads straight to bed. Lights out. No compromise.

When Dan takes a shower, it usually means an all-nighter is on the cards.

"Showering, I think." Despite the previous orgasm my vagina clenches, letting me know my body would be up for more, if I want it. And for some reason, tonight, I do. Something in the air is keeping the desire humming in my veins, more intensely than it normally does.

Will lets out a slow, harsh breath, and in that sound I can tell he's also aroused for a second time. Despite his age, my husband can occasionally surprise us both with his endurance.

"Hon, can you lean forward like that again, please? Hold the window ledge. Your cunt clenches when you're turned on and I want to be looking directly at it when he starts round two."

He's right. The part in question immediately clasps tight at his words and the already sensitized flesh throbs and aches.

The heady tang of his spent cum and the musky scent wafting from between my legs surround us with the titillating scent of sex. When I see the flash of his teeth as he grins it ignites an unexpected cascade of emotion. Butterfly wings beat gently against the walls of my stomach and I bite my lip, fighting sudden tears.

Why has he joined our sordid little game of voyeurism? It must be so difficult for Will to watch as I get turned on by another man. I know I'd hate it, if the situation were reversed. I *did* hate it, when I found out what he'd done at that conference. But am I not doing the exact same thing with Dan? Even though we've never actually met, never spoken, never touched, Dan and I are using each other's secret fetish needs to gain sexual pleasure from the experience in a way that could be construed as cheating.

I was so afraid, when Will uncovered my dirty little secret. Afraid that he would hate me, or think me disgusting, or somehow be completely turned off by my aberrant behavior. Equally scared that my saving grace might be taken away for good. *What if Will doesn't want me anymore? I couldn't bear it. And yet…what if I can never look at Danny again?*

I remember wanting to cry, mortified, but I was so afraid that if I started, I wouldn't be able to stop. *How can I possibly choose between the man I love, and the sexual urges I desperately need to fulfil?*

And yet I needn't have been concerned.

When Will told me he's turned on by what I've been doing, I heard his truth in the rough edge of his voice and the harsh inhale and exhale of breath.

Will. What am I going to do with you? Are we ever going to fully rediscover the happiness we shared only a couple of short years ago?

The truth is, since Will joined our little game I've been enjoying myself even more than before. The fact that my husband is willing to share this fantasy, and watch me, as I stand in the shadows watching Dan…

When our neighbor moved in five months ago, there was something about him that drew my attention, right from the moment I first saw him. Something about his self-confidence. His "*I don't give a shit what you think*" attitude. I couldn't stop looking at him, standing here in the darkness of our bedroom and wondering about the man in the apartment across the alleyway. How does someone become so uncaring of what others think?

I'd never seen anyone masturbate before. Never dreamed that someone would do it right in front of an open, lighted window.

Will probably did it, but never when I was around, and damn sure when he did he wouldn't have the light on and the blinds wide open. That look on Danny's face...

The way his mouth hung open, slack-jawed. The way his eyes were half-shut and his head thrown back in obvious enjoyment. One hand pulled at the rigid flesh of his cock while the other gripped the rounded end of some kind of implement that he'd reached behind to ease into his own ass. I'd never even *seen* another man's penis. Never in my whole life.

Oh my God. How big is that thing he's pushing up his bum? Does it hurt? Is he going deep? He's fucking himself into a frenzy.

I couldn't help it. I brushed my fingers over my mound and felt the flare of heat even through my plain cotton pyjamas as my body sizzled to life. It wasn't enough, to touch myself through my clothing. I needed to feel the slippery glide of my own juice, tease the swelling bud and then slide a finger into my creamy channel to find the sweet spot deep inside.

Encouraged by the exhibitionist nature of Dan's display, I began to touch myself in a sexual way. The first time ever I'd experienced sexual arousal from watching someone else. And after that first time, I was so intrigued I started waiting for him. And while I waited, I took off my pyjamas. Later, I added the heels.

Right now, though, I'm thinking about my husband, and a

smile curves my lips as I reach down to run a finger through the moisture leaking from my sex. I know my action will turn up the heat for Will. I swipe up and along my slit with a light feathery touch that mimics what Danny did to his companion and a shudder rattles through my body.

Are you watching this, Will? I lift a wet finger up to my mouth and trace my lips before slipping it inside to taste. Musky, yes. Also salty and creamy. No wonder they like to eat it out. *Do you want to taste this nectar?*

My husband lets out an agonized groan and the sound resonates deep inside my body. Those delicate butterflies become frantic, flapping furiously as a wave of elation leaves me trembling. For better or worse, Will is taking this crazy voyeuristic ride right along with me, and I couldn't be happier about this strange turn of events.

I love watching, but to know that, at the same time, someone is watching *me* in the throes of sexual passion...

To know that it's my *husband* watching me...

Yes. I love that, too.

CHAPTER 7

WILLIAM

Izzy bites her bottom lip and does as I ask, leaning toward the window and resting her hands on the sill, giving me a perfect view of her privates.

I *love* that view. There's a certain visual element that you just don't get when you're pressed up against your lover. While the skin-on-skin embrace might feel like heaven, you don't get to see and appreciate the little things like you can when you stand back and look.

Little things such as the way her pink vulva lips clench in and out as she waits, almost as if her channel entrance is breathing with a life of its own. Like the way her butt-hole looks like a tiny starburst just crying out for a finger to dip into its beckoning center. Like the way her dark hair cascading down her back turns a brighter, richer color in the glow cast by the street lamp. That same glow turns her pale skin almost radiant and smoothes away any imperfections.

Izzy is beautiful in so many ways that I would never have seen, never have appreciated, if it weren't for this time spent watching.

There's been a shift lately in how we're interacting. I'm

not sure how to explain it, except that I feel like things might be improving. That first night when I found her here, she had eyes only for our neighbor. Now she's aware of me too, and while she still likes watching him, it seems like maybe she's making room for me in this game.

She's aware of me now, and I think it heightens her pleasure to know that in a weird way we're kind of doing this together.

She's more patient than me when it comes to the waiting part, though. I can't see what's going on over there when I'm sitting down, and it's really hard not to rush over and push my greedy cock right between her legs. All I really want to do is touch my wife, then fuck her senseless. But on Sunday nights that isn't my role. Instead, I sit here and watch, learning how to appreciate the little things, and feel the slow burn in my groin build to an almost unbearable level.

I shift in the chair, occasionally touching myself to release the growing pressure. My balls are tight and hot, aching for release, and I grunt in relief when finally she blurts out, "He's back, Will. Looks like they've both showered. They're naked, and still wet, and...*oh*!" Her pelvis tilts in a squiggle of what appears to be excitement. "Looks like he's carrying the strap-on."

"Fuck yeah." An involuntary hiss escapes my lips and the burn intensifies. I could care less what the hell goes on over there. As long as Izzy is happy and aroused, I will be, too, and I know she loves it when that bastard brings out his toys.

The strap-on is a new favorite for Izzy. She says it's about the titillation of watching a woman with a cock step up and fuck a guy as virile and strong as Dan...

I can't deny it. The idea gets *me* horny as hell, too, and a drop of pre-cum squeezes out to decorate the head of my dick.

"She has the harness on already, Will. Looks like she's done this before."

Of course she has. The damn man certainly knows how to pick 'em.

I try and contain my snort, though. Izzy doesn't hate him the way I do. "Enjoy the ride, my love."

I stay quiet after that comment, sitting here in the shadows to watch, and after a couple of minutes she becomes engrossed once again in the activity in the opposite apartment.

"He's lying back on the bed, grinning from ear to ear." Her voice has the hoarse edge that always gives away the extent of her desire. "And, oh God, Will, she's leaning over to take him into her mouth. Deep. He's lying at a slight angle so I can see the ripple in her throat as he pushes into her."

I imagine this other woman kneeling beside the guy Izzy calls Dan, her hips encased in the leather harness strapping and an erect, dusky-colored penis jutting out from her snatch.

Is she hairless, like Izzy's current look, or does she have a bush that gives the cock a bed of hair to sprout from?

I wonder if her breasts are large and pink-tipped. I love Isabel's breasts, though she always gets so self-conscious about the effects of age and gravity.

When the woman leans down to take him into her mouth —hell, deep into her throat from what Izzy's saying—do those breasts swing back and forth as she works him hard?

Izzy lets out an agonized moan and I know things are heating up over there. What's going on? How hard is that woman working him? Is she as good as my wife at giving head? Or has she stopped using her mouth and started to fuck him instead?

"*Izzy.*" I can't help it. Her name whispers out of my throat in a groan of pleasure as I grip my cock and pull. The sensation is so intense my hips begin to buck and the chair starts its incessant squeaking. One day we'll replace it. But for now...

I groan again, and watch Isabel's fingers play briefly with her clit before her middle finger disappears up inside her channel.

The neighbor must love it. What guy doesn't? I wonder if he's a talker, with real words and phrases like "Fuck me", or "Suck me harder, you dirty little whore." I can't quite imagine it. I think he's more of a groaner like me. When Izzy sucks me off I can't string two words together. All I can do is moan and groan and release my load in her mouth, or sometimes all over her breasts.

CHAPTER 8

ISABEL

W hat does he taste like, my mirage lover? My tongue darts out to moisten my lips as I imagine taking him into *my* mouth. I will never know the reality, at least not with Diamond Dan, but my imagination works overtime to make up for it.

His companion finally comes up for air, and I see her swipe her thumb across his glistening tip and then smear the resultant moisture onto her fake cock. He leans up on one elbow and takes the head of it into his mouth, brief and shallow with his sucking. It's just a quick sampling of flavor that he licks away with an eager tongue before reaching up to squeeze the twin globes of her breasts.

She smacks away his hands and gestures firmly. He laughs in what looks like a wicked chuckle, and then he's rolling over to lay on his stomach between her straddling thighs.

There is a delicacy to her movements as she bends down onto all fours and lowers her pelvis toward his butt cheeks. She prods his crack with her toy and then uses her body to stroke it downward into the shadows between his legs, and then back up again where I can see.

Do you like that, Dan? Is it a turn-on to feel the hard flesh of another cock teasing you from behind?

She lowers herself further, laying right on top of him with the lower part of her body, while the upper part is held up by her forearms resting one each side of his ribcage.

His legs spread wide to accommodate her hips and she starts with tiny driving movements that grow in strength and frequency, until he too thrusts against the bed cover. His movements become so vigorous he lifts her with him into the air. Up and down, over and over, each of them thrusting and squeezing the bed clothes with tightly gripping hands.

A sudden movement from Dan and he is up again, this time on all fours, and his companion lines up her dick with the welcoming pucker of his ass. She hesitates, then says something, and he responds by reaching across to his bedside table and handing her a tube.

It must be lubricant of some kind. She smears some on the head of her toy, then holds the tube above his crack, letting more of it drip down into the seam. This joining is going to be wet and sticky.

He nods and she lines up again, then pushes hard until it's clear his tight muscles have relented and let her in.

His head arches back and I see the edge of his mouth stretching wide in a grimace. Does he not like the feeling of being breached in the ass? Is he moaning now, in pleasure, or in pain? Then I realize he is not grimacing. He's exhilarated, and the thought excites me almost into orgasm right then and there.

"Yes, fuck him," I urge as her hips begin to drive her cock home. He reaches between his legs and pumps his own organ as she thrusts hard into his ass.

The sight of her breasts jiggling as she holds onto his hips and pushes her way into the depths of his body is too much, and I feel the telling clench of an orgasm take hold and then push me over the edge.

I scream this time as I come, my breath fogging the window and my hands clutching the ledge. They come too, almost at the same time as me, and then I hear the tell-tale guttural moan from Will and I know without even looking that his second orgasm of the evening is arcing through the air in a spray of creamy cum.

I'm not even touching myself right now. I've moved my hands away to leave everything open and clear, so Will can see the spurt of fluid and the clench of my pussy as my body releases, my puckered little asshole squeezing tight, and the pulsing of my engorged clit as everything shatters at once.

Release. Agony. Ecstasy. Oblivion. Everything and everyone explodes until finally, all of us are spent.

I collapse against the window frame and a sob escapes. Too much. I can't even hold myself up any longer.

But then strong arms are there, supporting me, offering the love and comfort that I crave.

"Isabel."

Relief fills every fiber of my being as I turn and fall against him. Those strong arms of my husband hold me firm. "Will."

I can't even speak properly, I'm so spent, but I feel his grin break through against the top of my head and his lips press a delicate kiss on my scalp.

"Amazing. *You're* amazing. Your body, your total lack of restraint on these nights..." His arms tighten around me. "I can't get enough of watching you. Izzy, I *love* you."

The ferocity in his tone shocks me. I look up and into his eyes and read there just how much he means it. My butterflies are back, only now they're beating so hard against the walls of my stomach that the echo resonates right through my whole body. *This* is what it felt like when we were teenagers and Will first asked me out. I'd forgotten the giddy excitement and anticipation.

Only, right now it has nothing to do with sexual anticipation and everything to do with the anticipation of being held. Being *loved*.

I snuggle my head against his chest, and even though he's still wearing a shirt, the heat and the strength of his embrace is all-encompassing. He really loves me. I know it. I *feel* it in his touch.

"I love you too, Will. And I love that you get pleasure from this, well…fetish, I suppose it's called."

"Yeah. Course I do. You ready for bed yet?"

I nod. Danny will likely be done after that last performance. But even if he's not, for some reason tonight, *I'm* done. I need to go to bed with my husband, and I need him to hold me.

Touch. The one thing I will never have from Dan is the one thing I yearn for from my husband.

My arms snake around his waist and squeeze in return. His skin is warm and on this cold winter's night it is so reassuring to be in my husband's arms. "Take me to bed, Will."

I let out a huff of breath when he suddenly sweeps me up into his arms. My feet in those red stilettos dangle uselessly, and I rub my heels together, shucking them off. I don't need them anymore tonight.

He looks down briefly when they thump on the floor, then meets my gaze. "I love you in those heels, but I love you even more without them."

I wrap my arms around his neck. "Thank you." I'm not talking about the shoe comment, and he knows it. I see the knowledge in his eyes, and in the wry, self-deprecating grin that lifts his mouth at one corner.

"My pleasure, hon. I'm just glad...you know...that you found something to enjoy."

He lowers me to the bed, so much more gently than Dan did with his companion earlier in the night, and tucks me in before sliding in beside me. "As long as I get to keep doing *this*..." He slips one arm beneath my shoulders and wraps the other over my waist, spooning me tightly. "Then I'm a happy guy."

The realization hits in that instant, making me stiffen for a moment before relaxing into his embrace. "I'm happy too, Will."

Dan always sends his partners home and in the end he sleeps alone. I, on the other hand, am so much luckier. I get to do *this* every night. I nestle my backside into the curve of his body and my eyes drift closed. The best of both worlds. "I love it when you touch me, Will. When you hold me. When you...*love* me..."

The last thing I feel before the gentle drift into sleep is the tickle of Will's fingertips across my skin. Touch. The last taboo. And my husband does it to perfection.

CHAPTER 9

Last night was incredibly satisfying but it resulted in me sleeping through the alarm and now I'm running late for work. When you're in retail, it's important to get there in time to open the store. Or so my manager keeps telling me, whenever he rosters me on so early.

There's buttered toast in my mouth as I exit our building and I'm scrabbling through my purse for the car keys when I look up and...*he's* there. Danny. Standing right in front of me at the bank of mail boxes outside our building.

He's pushing a small padded envelope through the opening of one of the boxes, only he stops what he's doing when he sees me. I feel my eyes go wide and I'm positive I'm gaping. I glance down and back up. Yep. It's *our* mail box.

He's even more gorgeous up close, and I'm right about his eyes. They *are* blue, though I never got the full effect of their amazing heat until right now, when he's standing only three feet away and surprise turns them from brilliant aqua to a slightly darker hue.

My mouth drops open and I stand there like an idiot, until

I suddenly remember that the damn toast is still in my mouth. *Oh, my God.*

I quickly swallow then start to say something… anything…even just a simple, "Hi there." But I can't do it. The words stick in my throat like a wayward crumb from my food and won't come forth even when he lifts a slow hand toward my cheek.

Danny. Oh my Lord, are you really going to touch *me?*

My heart skips a beat then resumes its tattoo at a faster pace than before. For a second I think maybe he's going to do it. He wants to. I read the flare of longing in his eyes and wonder if he can see the same uncertain hunger reflected in mine.

The last taboo. His fingers almost graze one of the wavy clumps of hair that somehow always work loose from my hairclip no matter how diligently I try to tie it all back.

Will loves the bits of my hair that slip free. When he's off work and we sit together to watch television he's always playing with my curls, letting the strands slip and slide through his fingers as if it's a form of stress relief.

With Danny, though, it just doesn't seem right. I hold still, unable to bring myself to lean those final couple of centimeters toward him. Will we finally connect? Alarm wars with excitement and I'm not sure which side is winning. Something significant is about to happen and if I move a muscle, even to undertake a task as simple as breathing, it might destroy the perfection of the moment.

But then his hand drops away without touching me at all, and when the shift of air from his brief movement rustles across my skin, my shoulders sag and I know which side has won. *Relief!* My breath hisses out shakily and almost turns into a laugh when I hear the same hissing sound leave his lips.

Oh, Danny, my mirage lover. There are so many things I want to say to you. So many things I'd love to do with you. And yet I can't. We *can't. It would destroy everything we have. And I think you know it, too.*

His head dips to the side as he studies me in silence. I feel like his gaze is ravishing me, feature by feature, as he commits my image to memory. I know that's what he's doing, because I'm currently doing exactly the same to him. Then he nods once, his lips twisting in a crooked grin that acknowledges our unspoken connection.

We both realize at the same time that the package is still suspended half in and half out of our mail slot, held in place by his grip. Will he pull it out and hand it to me? He studies it, clearly considering, then with a sudden determined movement he pushes the envelope all the way in and it disappears inside the box.

Dan takes two steps away and pauses, then looks back at me again, his brows coming together in a quizzical frown. He opens his mouth, snaps it shut, and then he's gone, just that quickly.

I blink hard, swallowing down the regretful ache that still clutches at my throat. All the words that will never be said. All the actions that will remain forever in my imagination.

Oh, Danny. I can't yet bring myself to touch the post so I leave the box unchecked and continue toward my car. Whatever it is, it will be waiting there for me this evening. Perhaps it might be something I can wear during our sessions?

A sudden joy fills me. *I'm so lucky.* My husband, my real flesh-and-blood partner of over twenty years, continues to love me no matter what secret fetishes and desires lay beneath my ordinary façade. And I love him, too, despite what we've been through these past couple of years. He's the one who always holds me tight whenever I need it most. *He* is real. I know we'll get through this rough patch. I can already feel a lessening of the constriction that held me so cruelly in its grip when I first found out what he did.

Yet I also have my dream lover. My beautiful and "safe" mirage, Danny, who keeps me from starving in a world that doesn't always understand the desires that drive us.

Perhaps I am also Dan's mirage, in a way, and that's why he understood today when I hesitated. If you try to reach for a mirage and it turns out to be less than what you hope or expect...

Danny and I are correct not to break the fantasy by letting reality intrude, I'm sure of it. Will is my reality and I don't need anyone else to play that role.

This week I will continue to get on with life. My ordinary, extraordinary life. And next Sunday, at midnight, I will be waiting once again by the window, hoping to live out my voyeuristic fantasies and engage in a sensual game of watching where everyone who plays is a winner.

The End

I hope you enjoyed WATCH ME. Want more in the FORBIDDEN series? Keep reading for BREAKING THE RULES.

BREAKING THE RULES

A MÉNAGE ROMANCE

PREFACE

If you've always lived by the rules, how can you fall for two men who live to break them?

Stacey Gamble had it all. The perfect life, perfect partner, perfect children. Or so she thought. Until her husband had a mid-life crisis and ran off with their housekeeper, the kids decided to follow, and life as she knew it tumbled into ruins at her feet.

But that was okay. She picked herself up and began a new life – by the rules – in a quaint country town. Just to her liking. Alone.

Her new neighbors, Teale and James, throw a wrench into her plans. Literally. When the two sexy men rescue Stacey from a broken-down car in the dead of night, their offer of a three-some experience is far too tempting to resist.

Teale and James challenge Stacey's outlook and live-by-the-rules attitude. She soon finds herself in another crisis. A very provocative one.

And she isn't prepared.

Because if you live by the rules, you can't fall for two men who do everything to break them. Can you?

CHAPTER 1

STACEY

No one told me it gets darker out of the city than in. Like, pitch-black dark. I can barely even see my hand in front of my face, which is not a good thing when I'm sitting in a broken-down car in the middle of a country road. At midnight.

My two sisters said shifting to the country would be good for me. They said it would offer a fresh start, where I could forget all the shit that went down in the city and begin to move forward with my life. It all sounded very reasonable, and since moving here to this small rural oasis in the south-eastern part of Australia, I've finally been able to breathe once again.

I like the name of my new home. *Peaceton*. The town has a serene vibe that speaks to me in terms of what I'm looking for, and I haven't regretted my decision once in the four months I've been living here. Till this moment.

A street light or two would be nice. I check my mobile phone for the tenth time in three minutes and there's still no signal. Plenty of battery, mind you, because I never leave home without making sure my mobile is fully charged. The sensible one, my family call me. Always organized. Always prepared. Only, sensible does one no good at all if there's no phone signal. Apparently, my car broke down in a dead zone.

Awesome. So, I can sit here moping, or... Or what? What does one actually do in the country in this situation? It's too dark to identify any recognizable features so I'm not even sure how far I am from home. Close, I think, but...how safe is it to get out and walk? Are snakes more likely to come out at night? Are there dingoes—wild dogs—in this region? Are there...*serial killers* waiting to descend?

My heart is beating way too fast and I can't seem to draw in a proper breath. I'm pondering my best course of action in an attempt to rein in my too-vivid imagination, when a dark SUV drives past and then slows to a stop. The brake lights flash red, then the reverse lights come on and back up toward me until the vehicle sits idling right in front of mine.

Relief rushes through me, followed closely by trepidation when both the driver and passenger doors open and I realize the only weapon I have, if they turn out to be crazy nutters, is my handbag. Mind you, that's a pretty heavy-duty weapon. I flick on my headlights so I can see them a bit more clearly than my intermittent hazards allow.

A tall, lanky guy gets out the driver's side, and a slightly shorter but more heavily muscled man alights from the passenger side. Two guys, coming to my rescue. Two really fucking sexy guys, heading my way. My clit, a part of my body I thought long-dead, flickers to life with a throb. *I hope they're here to rescue me. I* hope *they're not serial killers.*

I crank my window about an inch and wait until they're both standing in front of it before I speak. "Hey." *Yeah, I know.* I'm not a great conversationalist at the best of times. This is not the best of times by a long stretch.

"Hey yourself," the lanky one answers in a lazy drawl,

and even though he's now out of the reach of my headlight beam so I can't make out his features properly, there's no mistaking the humor lacing his words. "Looks like you might need a bit of assistance."

I nod, realizing too late that they probably can't see my response in the darkened interior. "Yep. I definitely could use some help." Boy, my woman bits are really making themselves known all of a sudden. There's a steady throbbing between my legs and a pleasurable ache low down in my belly that I haven't experienced in a long time. I clear my throat. "I don't know much about cars, but I braked for that curve back there, and as soon as I took my foot off the accelerator the engine spluttered and died. Thank goodness I managed to steer it over here to the side of the road before it conked out altogether. Um...do you guys know much about cars?"

It annoys me that I sound like a stereotypical female, but the reality is, learning about car engines is not something that will ever be on my to-do list. I'm praying it might be an easy fix. I can't afford a big repair bill right now.

The muscled one lets out a snort. It sounds like he tried to muffle a laugh but didn't quite succeed, and my brows come together as I shoot him a look. "We know a bit." His voice is deeper than the driver's. There's a harsh edge to it that intrigues me. Are they local? Have I met them? They seem somewhat familiar.

"You're not out of gas?" At my negative response the driver nods at his companion, who heads back to their vehicle to retrieve what looks like a tool kit from the trunk. "Pop the lid and we'll take a look."

I do as they suggest, and after a few minutes of me sitting in the car staring blankly at my raised engine hood and hearing muffled bangs and mutters coming from somewhere in front of me, the muscled one is back at my window.

"It's no good. We're not going to be able to get you going tonight, but we can give you a ride home if you like, and help sort it out in the morning. We'll probably need to order in a part."

Home? How do they know…

"It's Stacey, isn't it?" Muscle man tips his head to one side as he queries me. "The soap woman."

The soap woman? I leave that one alone for now and squint into the dark. "Do we know each other… *Oh*! Are you my new next-door neighbors?"

The relief that floods my whole body has me sagging back against the seat. Until this second, I hadn't realized how on edge I was at the thought of being completely alone and helpless, if these guys turned out to be untrustworthy.

The taller, slow drawl guy is back too, and right on cue, the moon pops out from behind a cloud so I can see them a lot more clearly. *Holy heck, they're both so good-looking.* Two sets of high cheekbones, shadowed eyes, and wide, sensuous lips are revealed under the moon's silvery light. A double whammy of sex appeal where I least expect to find it. And yet each guy is quite different from the other. The one who got out of the passenger side is definitely heavier-set, with a tough edge lacking in the driver. His strong jaw hints at stubbornness, and those wide shoulders and narrow hips would look perfect at a weight-lifting event. The driver is attractive in a long, lean kind of way. Despite his slighter build and laid-back air, he seems like the more commanding of the two. I don't know why, but I get the impression he's the one in charge. His darkish hair is ruffled from whatever he did under my car hood, and my fingers itch to reach up and smooth out those wayward locks. As if he senses my desire to touch him, one corner of his mouth lifts in a quirky grin.

"Depends how you look at it," he answers. "We were there before you, so I guess you're *our* new next-door neighbor." I can still hear amusement in his tone so I'm positive he means no offence.

I hesitate, perhaps a moment too long for their liking. The bulkier one reaches into his back pocket and pulls out a wallet. "I'm James, and this is Teale Townsend." He gestures to his friend. "Here's my driver's license if you want to check our address."

He slides the plastic tab into the one-inch window gap and I shine my mobile light onto it. *James Castell.* His photo and the address match, but I don't really need it at this point. I recognize both of them now, even though the moonlight is still dim. I've seen them coming and going, albeit from a distance, between their house on the hill and a large garage built off to one side of their property. Now I understand why James laughed when I queried their car expertise. My guess is these guys run an auto shop. I couldn't have gotten luckier tonight if I'd won the lotto.

My little cottage is set back from the road and there's a couple of hundred meters between my place and theirs, but I've often watched them out of my kitchen window, wondering if they're in a personal as well as business relationship. Looking at the ease with which they stand together now, arms lightly touching as they wait for me to gather my bag and keys and open the door, I'm guessing yes. *Pity. Why are the sexy ones always off-limits?*

My clit hums again at the thought of watching these two go at it. An image of the two of them, sweat-streaked, naked, and rutting hard and fast, pops into my head and my breath hitches in my throat. *What is wrong with me?* It's been a while since I've had sex, I have to admit. Even before I found my husband in bed with the housekeeper, our relationship had been in decline for months. All in all, it's probably been over two years since anyone got near my hoo-ha. Maybe I'm just sexually frustrated. *I hope they can't sense it.*

I force deep breaths, in and out, trying to get my recalcitrant body back under control, and hand James back his license. "Thank you so much, both of you. I'd love a ride home if it's not too much trouble."

CHAPTER 2

TEALE

James and I have been watching her on and off in the four months since she moved here. Not in a creepy way, mind you, but just keeping an eye out for a window of opportunity to head on over and introduce ourselves. So far that opportunity hasn't arisen. I did make one attempt, about a week after she arrived, when I took across a batch of James' famous chocolate muffins. Boy, can that man cook. Lucky for me, cos I'd burn water if I tried. Unfortunately, our new neighbor wasn't home at the time, or maybe she just didn't want to come to the door. Word around town is that she's a bit of a recluse. Something bad happened in the city and she came out here to hide away.

Madge at the grocery store on Main Street says Stacey's not too social when she comes in for supplies. Apparently, she just wants to be left alone to get on with her soap-making business. Hearing that, we didn't want to encroach on her space so we never actually got around to meeting her in person.

There was something about her, that first day she arrived, that I can't even put my finger on. I was out in the garage, working on one of our client's cars, when I *felt* her presence. I can't explain it any different than that. She was just *there*, in our sphere all of a sudden, and something made me stop what I was doing and head on out to have a look. There was a small truck parked in the driveway next door, and a woman in faded jeans and an old grey T-shirt directed two men as they shifted pieces of furniture from the truck into the house. I couldn't tell from this distance how old she might be, or much of what she looked like. I could see that her hair was somewhere between brown and blonde, and it was shoulder-length and kind of messy. She looked pretty short, too, or else those delivery guys were extra tall. I had to fight the urge to head on over and wrap our new pint-sized neighbor in my arms to protect her. *From what?* No fucking clue, but this wasn't a feeling I'd ever had before, and I remember shifting from foot to foot, uncomfortable with my overly fanciful thoughts.

About that time, James came out on the porch and we exchanged a look. *Yeah.* Even from clear across the yard I could tell he had the same protective urge as me. He stood there a while, looking over toward the previously empty cottage as our new neighbor and her delivery guys toiled in the summer heat. At one point she stopped and raised her head, like a wild animal scenting the breeze, and then she turned and stared our way.

An instant connection flared. Unexplainable, and yet as real as anything I've ever felt. *Soul-mates.* Whatever it was disappeared as fast as it arrived, and then she lifted her hand in a tentative wave. James and I waved back in unison, and that's when we knew. Whoever this woman was, she was going to play a big part in our lives. At that point we just weren't quite sure how.

Now that I've had the chance to see her up close, meet her

properly, the connection is even stronger than it was that first day. She feels it too, I can tell. The scent of her desire fills my nostrils, and it's all I can do to keep control of my body. My cock is already halfway to hard, and when I glance at James and see the tightness across the front of his jeans, it mirrors my own. *Jesus.* We're like horny teenagers who can't keep our dicks in our pants.

She deserves more than that from us. I don't know what her story is, but I suspect she hasn't been treated right in the past. When she clambers into the back seat of my SUV, I glance over my shoulder and realize she's older than I first thought. *Good.* I'm not a fan of twenty-somethings who still have plenty of growing up to do. At a guess, I'd say she's only a couple of years younger than us, which would put her in her mid-thirties. Maybe it's her tiny frame that made me assume she was younger than that. Stacey's not classically beautiful, by any stretch, but there's some-thing about her that mesmerizes me. I don't know what it is. Her eyes, perhaps? They're big, and blue, with the longest lashes I've ever seen on a woman. But her eyes reflect sadness, even as she smiles her thanks, and there's a tightness in the skin around them that hints at contained emotion. Eyes as beautiful as that should never hold grief or stress.

What's your story, Stacey? Where did you come from? Why are you so sad?

James turns in his seat and they chat while I concentrate on driving. It's not far, only a few miles, but this stretch of road winds quite a bit with a couple of tight hairpin bends. At night in particular you have to watch out for wombats or kangaroos crossing in front of you. Hit one of those, even with a vehicle as sturdy as mine, and no one comes out unscathed.

Her voice is soft and soothing, and I enjoy eavesdropping on their conversation.

"You called me the soap woman," she says at one point, and James chuckles.

"That's what they call you in town."

"Really? Well, I suppose it's accurate, in a way. I make my own soaps and body lotions and I sell them, mostly online but sometimes at local markets."

"Cool. I know where to go for my next lot of family Christmas presents, then."

"By all means, James." She laughs and the light sound fills our car, and my heart, with a sense of joy. I could listen to that laugh all night long. "I'll have to give you both a significant discount after this, won't I? Thanks again for the ride. I really appreciate it, guys."

I grunt, wanting in on the conversation. Feeling a hint of jealousy that she's directing all her attention toward James. "It's no problem, Stacey. We were on our way home from a catch-up with friends, so it isn't out of our way at all. We'll have your car towed in the morning, and get it running again before you know it."

"Thanks. I got doubly lucky tonight, didn't I?"

Her words echo into a silence that is suddenly charged with hidden meaning. She coughs as if embarrassed, and leans back in her seat, and none of us speak again until we reach her place. When we pull up in front of the house, Stacey's security lights come on, illuminating the yard in a blaze of silvery-white brighter even than daylight. *What the hell?* I hide my grin at her city habits, certain she's got her door locked and probably dead bolted too. Half the time James and I don't bother to secure the place at all when we leave home, but I guess that's a product of us growing up here in Peaceton where everyone knows everyone else's business.

Besides, no one would dare steal from us. They'd risk a pummeling from James.

Stacey slides out of the back seat and I'm not sure whether to follow. Is this the end of our interaction? I've hardly said more than a couple of words. It isn't enough. Not nearly enough. James hesitates too, and I can tell he's debating whether or not to jump out of the car.

Then she turns back to face us and her shoulders firm as if she's steadying her nerves. "Teale. James. Would you like to come in for a quick nightcap? Just to say thank you. You know, for the ride."

The security light is so bright it washes everything silver so I can't tell if she's blushing or not. I'm guessing she is by the way her eyelids flick down and up in an embarrassed-looking flutter, and her words tumble out so fast it takes a couple of seconds to process what she's asking.

This woman makes me want to laugh, and hug her, and fuck her, all at the same time.

James is out of the car before I can even think about formulating a response. Too bad if I decide we should take things slow. He shoots me a look, almost challenging, and after a moment I nod. *Yeah man. I get it. You want her. Me too.* But no matter what James thinks, I'm going to make damn sure we don't do anything about it, tonight or any night, unless Stacey wants it too.

As I follow them inside, my hands shake and my stomach does a series of painful flip-flops. I don't know anything about this woman other than the barest minimum of facts, but I'm absolutely certain about one thing. Somehow, James and I need Stacey Gamble in our lives.

CHAPTER 3

STACEY

I can't believe I've invited them in. What is wrong with me? They might live next door, but they're still practically strangers. How is it even possible to be sexually attracted to two men, both at the same time? It isn't like I have the urge to be with one, and then the other, on different occasions. My mind is filled with images of the two of them, together, like a package deal or something. I have the strangest sense you wouldn't get Teale without James, or vice versa. You'd get both, and the titillation of that knowledge sends my sexual craving into overdrive.

They're just so...connected. That's the only word I can think of when they make themselves comfortable on the adjustable bar chairs at my kitchen bench. I don't even know why I'm imagining being the meat in a James and Teale sandwich. They're clearly a couple, and I'm obviously having some kind of deviant breakdown due to anxiety.

A ménage encounter. Why am I obsessing over that idea, for the first time in my life? Why can I not stop wondering what it would be like if one of them laid me out right here on the kitchen counter top and held my legs wide so the other could lean in and taste my hungry sex?

Slick moisture dampens my panties and I turn to the sink to hide my need. I busy myself filling the kettle with water and switch it on to heat up. Can they sense my desire? Can they smell it? Can they see it in my eyes when I take a deep breath and turn to face them once again? "Do you want tea? Coffee? Or something stronger? I have beer if you prefer, or wine?"

A ménage experience isn't something that's ever crossed my mind before, but right now it seems to be the only thing I can think about. Yep. My thoughts are making me blush.

James stares hard at me, his gaze intense. He's the darker of the two in coloring, with tanned skin, brown hair, and the most amazing eyes. They're brown too, but so dark they border almost on black. The depth in those eyes is quite unreadable and strangely mesmerizing. His silence draws me in, causing my lips to part and my breath to shorten. I want to leap over the bench and kiss him.

Teale swings a little on the swivel chair and breaks the silent spell cast by his partner. He is lighter in color, his brown hair tipped attractively with blonde and his eyes are a smoky grey that change to green and back when I shift my gaze to his. The changing eye color is disconcerting. It is equally as mesmerizing as looking at James, but in a completely different way. Teale's gaze somehow demands respect. He's an intriguing contradiction, both laid back and commanding. His very presence makes me feel infinitely safe and yet, contrarily, in imminent danger of being ravished.

As I study him, a slow, seductive smile transforms his features from severe to sensual, and it takes my breath away. *Oh, Teale.* When he speaks I'm still so fascinated by the contradictions he presents that it takes time to process what he's saying. *How is it possible to find two such different men equally attractive? What is it about these guys that steers my thoughts in such a decadent direction?*

He speaks again and I shake my head. "Um, sorry, what was that?"

Teale's grin widens. "I said, I'd love a beer, thanks."

James lets out a grunt. "Me too, if that's okay?"

I blink, no doubt looking like an idiot. "Fine by me. It's kind of too late for coffee anyway." I switch off the kettle and retrieve three beers from the fridge. Might as well join them, I guess. And it gives me a couple more minutes to try and re-compose myself while I get the tops off the bottles. "Cheers, guys."

We clink and drink, me standing on one side of the kitchen counter, them sitting on the other. I'm not usually a beer person, preferring wine when I do drink alcohol. My ex-husband says beer is for rednecks and toward the end of our relationship he only drank red wine, so there's a contrary little voice in my head that keeps saying I have to keep a six-pack in the fridge for visitors, just to spite him. He'll never know, of course, but *I* know, and it feels like proof that I can now do whatever the hell I want. I'm out from under that bastard's control, and if I want to drink goddamn beer, I *will*.

The first sip goes down smoothly, leaving a pleasant yeasty tang on the back of my throat. Yum. Maybe I'll become a regular beer drinker. A true country gal. I take a bigger sip and choke a little. *Okay, maybe not.* This time it's James who smirks. He leans across to wipe a wayward drip of liquid from the edge of my lips and it's all I can do not to turn my head and suck his thumb deep into my mouth. *How do I stop these cravings?*

"How long have you been a couple?" These guys are seriously off-limits and somehow, I have to remember that. "You look very comfortable together."

Teale raises a brow and exchanges a quick look with James before he answers for both of them. "We're not exactly gay, Stacey."

Wait, what? My heart skips a beat as the protection of them being lovers is stripped away.

"We live together, of course. Have done for...what? Nine or ten years now? Since I inherited the house from my grandmother in my late twenties."

James nods and Teale continues. "We were already working together in the auto business, and it made sense to move the shop into the ready-made garage on the property. Used to be a stable block, a long time ago, so it didn't take a lot of remodeling to make it work for us. We're walking distance from Main Street so our customers can still get here easily, but now we save on rent."

James pipes up. "Once we had the business re-established there, Teale was kind enough to invite me to live in, too. It made sense. We get on well. Always have, even back in high school."

Best friends. Not lovers? "I'm sorry, I just assumed—"

"You're not completely wrong, actually." James tilts his head to study me, as if curious about my reaction. "We *are* lovers—occasionally—but more often it'll be in a ménage arrangement with a woman we both like."

"*Oh!*" There can be no doubting my reaction. My cheeks are so hot I must look like a pickled beetroot. Just like that, they've stripped away everything I thought I knew about myself and what I'm willing to accept in a relationship. My sex is aching and full at the discovery that these guys really do live outside the rules of convention. *Threesomes. They like threesomes.* "You mean...you sleep with the same woman... at the same time?"

"Does that shock you, Stacey?" Teale's voice is gentle; slightly teasing.

I shrug and shake my head, trying to appear cool but knowing that he sees right through my guise. I'm *not* cool with this. I don't understand the whole ménage thing. How do the participants not get jealous? How do they make sure everyone gets what they need, both physically and emotionally? How do they make sure nobody ends up feeling left out? Most importantly, how do they stop everyone else outside the relationship judging and looking down their noses because their sex life isn't considered *normal*?

I don't understand my own body's intense reaction to the idea of sex with both Teale and James at the same time. I *crave* normal, especially after my experiences over the past couple of years. A threesome is not something I'm personally familiar with, or have ever sought out, and it's certainly not something I'd ever consider the *norm*. Right now though, my traitorous clit swells and my cunt is damp as my mind floods with images of Teale, James, and now me in the mix too, rutting and pleasuring each other in combinations only limited by my imagination.

By the way, I have a *vivid* imagination.

Finally, I manage to answer Teale. "No." *Liar. They don't deserve that.* I take a deep breath and try again. "Well, yes but..." I stop, completely confused by the strength of my physical craving. What will happen if I admit we're on the same wavelength? Most likely something I'll seriously regret tomorrow. But if I let these sexy men walk out of here, without being truthful about the need rising within me by the second, I think I might regret that even more.

What the heck? There's no one who could possibly be

hurt by my actions. Not anymore. My ex-husband lives in Perth, clear on the other side of Australia, and our twin boys are with him for now. They prefer his luxury beachside mansion to my rustic little cottage in the country and to be honest, who could blame them?

No one to know. No one to pass judgement, except the three of us right here in this room. My heart is thudding so hard it feels like it's about to burst right through my ribcage. "I...I want..." They're so patient with my fumbling hesitation, but even so I can't quite bring myself to say it. My mind is humming with so many *if's, but's,* and *maybe's* I can't think straight at all. It's like I was protected from my own imaginings when I thought these guys were a couple. Now that I know they're seriously into sharing their women, there's nothing between the decadence of my ménage fantasies and the possibility of making it real.

Nothing, other than the very narrow divide of this sturdy kitchen bench. I swallow hard, and allow James to remove the bottle of beer from my suddenly nerveless fingers.

"We want you, Stacey." James's voice is soft, but I hear the thrum of need running beneath the words. It ramps up my own desire a thousand times over. My clit heads past a dull ache into full-on throbbing, and my throat is tight as I swallow again, trying to hold in the moan that wants to escape.

Teale stands and moves around the bench until he's directly behind me. His light breath warms the back of my neck and his firm body molds around mine from the rear. He has a hard-on. An unmistakable, very *big* hard-on that is clearly straining for release from those jeans. "We want you *a lot,*" he says, confirming the comment from James.

No kidding.

Teale splays his hands on the bench, one each side of me,

and just like that I'm imprisoned in a human cage. He shifts, leaning down to whisper further words in my ear. His breath tickles, sending shivers right through my body. "We won't do anything unless you want this too, Stacey. *Do* you? Want this?" He thrusts with his pelvis, crushing my mound into the edge of the bench. My breath hisses out at the decadent sensation. *Pain, and pleasure.* "You're gonna have to admit it, gorgeous. Out loud."

I don't know these men; have never met them officially before tonight, and logic tells me I should be terrified of this situation and ask them to leave my home. But I don't want to let them go. I want to feel desirable again, to someone. And these two men are making it abundantly clear that in this situation, *both* of them desire me. I want to remember what it feels like to be loved. I want *sex*, damn it, for the first time in far too long.

And if the men in question are as sexy as Teale and James, I want this with every fiber of my being.

I look up and James is watching for my reaction. The rampant need in his eyes flares even brighter when he reads my affirmative response. He's already standing up when I shift awkwardly in the cocoon of Teale's arms, turning to face him. Teale's cock presses directly against my clit.

Oh mama. That feels so fucking good. "Yes." *Time for truth.* "I do want this, Teale. I want you and James right here, right now. More than I've ever wanted anyone or anything in my life."

CHAPTER 4

JAMES

The second I receive Stacey's unspoken permission I'm out of my seat like a jackrabbit with a terrier on its tail, even before she confirms out loud what I've already seen in her eyes. I can't reach her fast enough. Can't even wait to get around the bench. Instead, I lean forward over the tiled counter top and slide my hands under her armpits to lift her up and onto the hard surface. I try to be gentle, but I'm trembling from the depth of my need and it's difficult to hold onto control. Teale's still joined with her, cock to cunt, with only the thin layers of their clothing keeping them from consummating the connection. My breath is rapid and my heart is pounding in my chest. I don't remember ever feeling this level of anticipation in the past.

I urge her backward until she's lying face up with her sexy-as-fuck legs wrapped tight around Teale's already thrusting hips. He moves with her, his hard-on positioned perfectly right there at the heart of her pussy mound. When he raises his head to look straight at me, just for a second or two, I can tell he's as eager as me to pleasure this beautiful woman splayed out between us. This close the green of his eyes is almost emerald. No grey left at all in that penetrating stare. They only turn that rich bright color when he's in the midst of intense emotion. We share a quick grin, a tacit acknowledgement that we each recognize the need of the other, and then I focus once again on Stacey. Her wide mouth is parted and her expression slightly startled, but the desire I saw in her eyes hasn't waned. If anything, it ramped up even more.

I run my thumb down the side of one cheek and around her jawline, enjoying the softness and heat of her skin. She has a nice, sort of heart-shaped jawline that suits her tiny build. Her hair splays out across the bench surface in a tangled light brown mess. When I sink my fingers into it, a subtle perfume is released into the air and I bend my head to take in the scent. *Delicious*. Her face in the middle is delicate-looking, her lush lips curved into a timid and enticing smile. She reaches up a hand and cups my cheek.

"Did you guys somehow read my mind?" Her voice is husky, so soft that I have to lean in even closer to hear her, and as I do the tip of her tongue flicks out to moisten those lips. I can't deny their sensual call any longer, and I kiss her despite the awkward upside-down positioning of our mouths. As soon as I do, I'm gone.

My God, this kiss. When our mouths connect, a spike of fire shoots straight to my groin. My cock was already halfway to heaven, but now I'm about to burst at the seams. My jeans, which were admittedly snug a minute or two ago, are so restricting it's painful. I've rarely kissed anyone upside-down like this, and it feels weird and far sexier than I was expect-ing. We tease at first, in a delicate dance of lips and tongues and teeth, parting and reconnecting as we begin to learn each other. She's good at this, if a bit hesitant at first, but as our kiss goes on, something in the connection changes and I feel her confidence grow. My tongue dips in and out, meeting hers in a sensual caress that draws us in even further. A tiny moan, almost a whimper, erupts from her throat directly into mine, and then she opens her mouth fully to let me in. I drink in her gorgeous essence. Her scent, her texture, her taste.

Stacey. You taste so fucking good. You feel *so fucking good.*

I'm drowning in this experience. I can't think; can only taste. Can only feel. I'm lost in the depths of an incredible kiss. Lost in the gentle swell of her breasts beneath my exploring hands. Lost in the tiny moans and groans and the tremors that shake her body beneath my touch. I completely forget Teale, until strong fingers slide into my hair and pull. Hard.

Fuck. How is that possible? I've never forgotten Teale before, no matter who we're with. He and I take our enjoyment with whoever happens to be on hand and yet always, we remain a team of two with a temporary third allowed in to the mix. Stacey's earlier assumption about us as a couple is at least partially correct. Only this time it's different. So different. This time Stacey is firmly at the center and there's no question that this is an equal threesome. This time it feels like a proper *ménage a trois*. Maybe for the first time ever.

Teale tugs again at a hunk of my hair, using more force than is needed to pull my head up and away from our woman. He's pissed. He knows I forgot him and he doesn't like it. He leans forward over Stacey and kisses me, brief and hard. It's a vigorous reminder of his presence in a way I can't ignore, his kiss overlaying the subtler presence of Stacey, until my lips throb from their combined attention and my cock is so hard and hot I'm ready to blow.

Once Teale has made his point with me, he swoops down

to take my place with Stacey, claiming her lips with a kiss that looks every bit as sexy as mine felt. A flare of jealousy shards my chest, especially when her arms twine up around his neck and they're completely connected from lips to hips. He's still thrusting, the movement sending her sliding back and forth across the counter top, and those moans coming from Stacey confirm how much she's enjoying it.

From one moment to the next I'm out of the loop, a superfluous third wheel, and the flicker of hurt puzzles me. We do this all the time, Teale and I, sharing the same woman. It's our *thing*. Makes everything that little bit more exciting. We've done it since our last year of high school when a drunken night out resulted in our first time together sexually and we finally understood what being bisexual meant. Within weeks we both developed a crush on the same older woman, and from the moment we took her, together, we haven't looked back. Us against the world. Together forever.

I've never felt like this before, as if there's an emotional connection with Stacey beyond the physical, and if I can't be an equal part of it with Teale I'm going to be left behind. Confusion builds, and I don't know what to do. They're really going at it. Stacey's legs are wrapped so tight around Teale's hips that, despite the protection of clothing, they already look like they're physically joined. He's pounding into her, at first slow and steady and then increasingly more frenzied.

I want that prime position between her legs. *I* want to feel that rhythmic pressure and squeeze against my cock. I want to take it all the way, driving deep into her channel to feel the tight pull as her vaginal muscles milk me for everything I have. *Jesus. I have to fuck this woman before I explode in my trousers.*

I ready myself to return Teale's favor and yank his head up and away from her, when one of her arms unravels from around his neck and flutters up toward me. Her hand flaps blindly, clearly in a search for mine, and I grip her tightly, lacing our fingers together. *She wants me too.* Just like that, I'm no longer on the out and my heart skips a beat and resumes extra fast at the anticipation of what is about to occur.

Teale breaks off their kiss and scoots down her body, until his mouth is positioned right at the juncture of her thighs. I've experienced that hot breath on my dick and I know what it probably feels like for her right now, even through the fabric of her jeans. Her lips are swollen from kissing both of us and she's panting hard as if she's been running. When he drops a kiss onto her mound, using his teeth in a scraping bite across the denim, there's no doubting whether or not she can feel it. Her back arches off the bench and she lets out another of those mewling sounds. It sends a signal straight to my cock.

I want this woman so bad.

Teale unzips her jeans and begins to shimmy them down over her hips, so I follow his lead and do the same with her top. It's pretty. Black and white with little red flowers scattered across it, and briefly I wonder where she went tonight, before her car broke down. *A date?* If so, why did he leave her to get home alone?

The thought dissipates into nothing as her top comes off. Holy *shit*, but she has beautiful skin. It's smooth and pale, dotted here and there with tiny freckles, and against that lacy black bra and panties she looks good enough to eat. Thank *fuck* her bra unfastens at the front. My fingers are too unsteady to deal with anything complicated. I unsnick the hook and slide that off too, just as Teale rips her panties down her legs, and then she's lying naked across the counter top with arms and legs akimbo. Her erect pink nipples, enticing curves and that moist slit between her legs add fuel to my already out of control fire.

She lays there. Trembling. Waiting. Silently begging for whatever we choose to do next.

CHAPTER 5

TEALE

S he's so fucking gorgeous. Now that she's naked I can't stop looking at her. Her skin's so pale, dusted here and there with a few stray freckles, and her curves are subtle, matching her pint-sized build perfectly. Not a big-breasted woman, which is fine by me, because right now I have my mouth between her legs and all I want to do is taste her beautiful cunt.

There's a subtle scent that fills my nostrils, a little like lemon and the freshness of eucalyptus leaves. Reminds me of the Australian outdoors. Maybe it's one of the lotions she makes for her online store? Whatever it is, the fragrance is so delicious it entices me like no other scent I've ever known. Her pussy is hairless and I'm grateful as it gives me a better view of her seam and all it contains. Her slit is shiny with moisture and I haven't even started, yet. I use my tongue to trace up one fleshy lip and down the other side. Tiny goose bumps form in the wake of my tongue's journey, and I thank fuck she's a modern woman who likes to remove most of her bush. Makes it so much easier to tease at her clit and her channel entrance until she makes that debauched moaning sound and sends my own erection into overdrive.

I blow on her clit, circling the prominent rosy button with my finger tip but not quite touching it. She arches into my hand as if straining for more. A keening sound surrounds us and for a moment I'm distracted. *Is that James?* I was nasty to him before, cutting him out like that, but the flare of jealousy that pierced my chest when I saw how much she enjoyed his kiss was mind-blowing. I wanted in on that. I wanted to remind them both that I'm here too. *I'll make it up to you soon, James. I promise.*

Then I realize it isn't James but Stacey making that inhuman noise. She's contorting her body in an attempt to reach my hand or mouth. I relent and allow my thumb to graze lightly across her clit. Her violent shudder galvanizes me into action and I connect with her wet seam in an intimate kiss, licking and sucking and tasting. Her flavor is every bit as delicious as its promise. I find her vaginal entrance and plunge my tongue deep inside before sliding back out and up to reclaim her clit. Unlike most women I've been with, she has a bud that protrudes beyond her pussy lips, and I love that I can suck the whole thing right in to my mouth, working it as delicately and thoroughly as I would the tip of James' cock. It swells in my mouth even more as my exploring fingers take advantage of the slickness left behind by my tongue to find and penetrate her channel.

She arches up again, this time in a bucking motion that continues beyond the initial thrust. I ride the movement with her, keeping that clit firmly embedded in my mouth, flicking it with my tongue and sucking hard. Clutching fingers reach into my hair, the frantic grip urging me to go deeper; harder. She's so wet. So slick. So ready.

I slide a second finger inside her, and then a third. Her

heat settles around me as I drive in and out in a rapid finger fuck that causes another loud wail to rip out of her. Her scent rises and I'm sinking ever deeper into its intense aroma. The scent of sex, and the fresh outdoors, and something I'm beginning to identify as uniquely Stacey, has me hovering right on the edge of release even though I'm still fully clothed.

James, too, is close to orgasm. I can tell by the desperation in that low groan he releases. The sound mirrors Stacey's, and I glance along her body to see him bent over her breasts, moving back and forth between them like a starving man presented with two favorite foods. His hips are thrusting jerkily against the edge of the counter top as he licks and sucks first at one of her nipples, and then the other, and back again. Her nipples are erect, the central buds pointing toward the ceiling and coated in shine from James' oral attention. From this angle, looking up from between her legs, those shiny nipples are one of the most erotic things I've ever seen. I can tell by that glazed look in James' eyes that he's fully focused on what he's doing, suckling at each breast in turn and kneading the soft curves of flesh.

James is muscled and hard, far more heavily built than me, but I've felt those hands on my own body at times and I know how skilled and gentle he can be. He's good at teasing, an expert at subtlety of touch, and I'm grateful he's using that expertise on Stacey. She's trembling from head to toe and her hands clench and unclench by her sides as if she can no longer control herself at all.

Good. Time to tip her over the edge.

I return to her pussy and her clit, licking and sucking hard. From one second to the next her moan becomes a shriek and her back arches up as a rush of heat fills my mouth. The pulsing contractions of her climax begin to vibrate against my lips. *Yes, beautiful Stacey. Fall into it. Let yourself go.*

Stacey

Oh yes. The agony. The ecstasy. The onslaught goes on and on from what feels like every direction, until I can't hold it in and I'm gone, shuddering and shrieking beneath their combined attack in an orgasm more intense than anything I've ever experienced in my life.

There's nothing but sensation. It rolls through me in huge, mind-blowing waves, throwing me deep into the black, into nothing. Eventually, the waves become smaller and I slowly drift back to reality. I'm spent, sprawled across the kitchen counter top like a deadweight, with Teale's eyes glinting up at me from between my thighs and James breathing hard above me. The latter's lips are curved in a fierce triumphant smile.

I shift and stretch, letting out a groan when muscles I didn't even know existed make their presence felt. I'm going to be sore tomorrow. This hard kitchen bench is an unforgiving place for sex, as I've just discovered.

Teale straightens and glances around. "Which way's your bedroom, Stace?"

He seems tense. So does James. If they're as much in need of an orgasm as I was, I have no idea how they're still holding on at all. I gesture toward the rear doorway. "Down the hall. It's the last room on the right." How am I going to make it there when my legs are still shaking and my body is lethargic from such a powerful climax? I struggle to sit up and let out a yelp when James scoops me into his arms. He does it easily, as if I weigh nothing. I let trust take over, relaxing into his firm chest as he carries me down the hallway.

Teale precedes us, opening my bedroom door and leading the way into the room. Thank goodness I tidied it this morning as I do every Saturday, changing the sheets and picking up all the stray bits of clothing that seem to appear out of nowhere over the course of the week. James deposits me gently on my king-sized bed, a luxury that seemed silly when I purchased it, but now with three of us I wonder if something was guiding me that day at the furniture store. Maybe I knew deep down that I was destined for a ménage experience? My fanciful thoughts freeze and the moment becomes charged with tension as I sit up and come face to face—quite literally—with the extent of their physical need.

Two erections at eye height, both squashed tightly into jeans in a way that must be highly uncomfortable. I can see the outline of their organs and a patch of damp on Teale where he's likely pressed himself into my sex while I was splayed out on the bench. Is that my wet heat, or his pre-cum? My body, still aching from my orgasm only a couple of minutes ago, is suddenly ready for more. *How is that possible? How is it that I still need more from these men?*

"Teale. James. It's time for you to get undressed and join me." My order comes out so husky I don't even recognize my own voice. *Who am I tonight?* I tilt my head, waiting for their response, and then lie back against the pillows to watch as they do my bidding.

James is ready first, ripping off shoes, shirt, and trousers in record time without regard for buttons or zippers. His cock springs free when he shimmies off black boxer briefs, and for a few moments I'm riveted by the impressive sight. His tip is helmeted, already shiny with leaking pre-cum fluid, and his organ is thick and hard, matching his build perfectly. My vagina clenches involuntarily at the thought of all that rigid flesh inside me. I can't wait.

Eventually, I break free of my hypnotic fascination with his cock and my greedy eyes have a chance to drink in the rest of his superbly crafted body. There's no doubt in my mind he must work out at a gym. *Is* there a gym in Peaceton? It's no wonder he lifted me so easily. His shoulders are wide and hips are narrow, with skin evenly tanned all over, including his arse which I notice when he gives a cheeky little twirl. There are attractive indentations in each butt cheek that my fingers ache to reach out and caress.

But first, we need Teale to join us. I turn my attention to the other man in the room, urging him with my eyes to hurry. He's far more considered in his movements than James, undressing slowly and taking time to fold his jeans before placing them on the small chair in the corner. His shirt comes next, button by slow button, and if I didn't know better I'd say he was reluctant to join us. But the burning color of those eyes tells a different story, and I suspect he's drawing out the anticipation in his own contrary way. When he lowers his underwear to reveal a massive, almost vertical erection that looks like a volcano about to blow, there's no doubting how much Teale wants this too.

My impatience flares. "Come on, Teale. Get over here."

"He's always like this. It's just his way."

I love that James is trying to protect his friend and ensure I don't get annoyed at the pedantic pace. I let out a laugh. It sounds breathless and I concede Teale's snail pace has ramped up my eagerness. And my nerves. "At least it gives me time to enjoy the view."

James chuckles. "I agree wholeheartedly."

I glance at him and my breath stops in my throat. James isn't looking at Teale. He's staring at me with such appetite that for a moment I'm almost afraid. This excited expectation is so powerful, so unlike anything I've ever experienced, my response borders on panic. I'm terrified and exhilarated at the same time. I don't understand the strength of my feelings, nor the underlying cause, but I do know I feel more *alive* in this moment than I've ever felt before.

For the first time in forever, I'm living in the moment rather than calculating right or wrong. This experience just *is*. I can't explain it any more accurately than that. Craving rushes through my veins, reaching every part of my body and centering in my cunt. In minutes I'll have both of these men embedded deep inside me. The thought should send me scurrying, but it doesn't, even as doubts assail me.

What if they're too big? What if it hurts? What if I don't like it? What if I do like it? What if I like it so much that I can't ever stop? It doesn't matter what my brain throws at me. When James climbs onto the bed behind me, and Teale steps forward to stare down at us both, I know that this is what I need.

Teale's hunger rages as fiercely as mine. It is evident in the tightness of his features, in his hands clenched into fists by his sides. In the dark red, purple veined hard-on calling out for attention right in front of my face.

I tentatively reach out and take him in my fist and he lets out a long low groan. Unlike James and I, it's the first sound Teale has made that betrays his sexual need, and I *love* it. I want to make him groan again. I run my hand up and down his hot flesh, fast and then slow and fast again, until he shudders and a spurt of fluid from the tip wets my hand and creates a slippery, slapping sound when I pull. Another groan erupts from Teale, low and heartfelt. The sound is as effective as a finger or tongue on my clit, and now it's my turn to clench my muscles tight and hope for eventual release.

James is breathing unevenly behind me and I want to include him too. Keeping hold of Teale's cock, I carefully encourage him onto the bed beside me before twisting a little so I can take James's erection into my other hand.

Two hands, two cocks. Two impressive erections, and twice the slick, wet pleasure as I glide my fists up and down, learning their uniquely different shapes. Surrounding myself in the very male and enticingly delicious aroma of sexual need and cock juice.

Now that I'm sandwiched between them on the bed and James starts to explore my body with one hand, I realize Teale's slow deliberation reminds me of a predator stalking its prey. He's so damn sexy in that unhurried way he moves, and even though he's still not touching me—yet—my stomach is churning and my whole body is once again on fire as I realize this is *it*. This is the moment I'm about to pop my virginal threesome cherry.

Teale throws something discreetly across to James. Condoms. And a tiny tube of lubricant. *Ah*. Makes sense that Teale is the boy scout of the two. My nerves increase at the reality of what they're about to do.

"Are you okay?" *Now* he touches me, and his hands are confident and sure. He rolls me onto my side so I'm facing James, and tucks smoothly in behind me.

James re-positions himself more comfortably in front. I've already imagined us like this, and somehow even before this moment I knew Teale would take the rear. The reality is quite different to my fantastical imaginings though. I feel their every breath, in and out, like a vibration against my own ribs. Their spicy scent envelops me. Their hard-ons are mashed up against me with a kiss of wet wherever they touch. Two sets of hands caress my body as if eager to learn every inch, wandering over my breasts, across my hips and further down. Exploring fingers dip into my slit from both front and rear and I struggle to keep my pelvis still.

"You're dripping." James speaks in a low hard tone, and I can't tell if he thinks my wetness is a good thing or not. My ex-husband hated that about me. He said it was disgusting, as if I'd wet the bed when we had sex. My cheeks flare with heat at the memory and I push at James' hand.

"I'm sorry, I can't help—"

"We love it, Stace." Teale's voice is a sexy whisper in my ear. His breath tickles my neck and sends a shiver across my suddenly over-sensitized skin. "The wetter the better. In fact, the more wet you are, the hornier I get. I want to fuck you so hard, baby. But I won't. Not this time. The first time, we'll be gentle, I promise. Especially me, in *here*."

I feel one of his fingers caress my anal entrance and, far from frightening me off as I expect, the touch ignites weird sensations that send a signal straight to my clit. *Yowza! That feels good.* I'm entering new territory here. My breath is so short I'm afraid I'm about to hyper-ventilate.

"Relax honey." James tips my chin up until I'm staring straight into his intense chocolate-colored eyes. "Teale's the best at this. He'll take you so gently you'll be begging him to go harder. And any time you want us to stop, just say so." He shifts a lock of hair across my forehead and smiles. The tender gesture—and his words—comfort me.

I take a deep breath and let it out slowly. Again, and then again, until I feel less light-headed. "Better get to it then, gents. Before I come without you. Yet again."

Their laughter is quiet and fills me with renewed confidence. This *is* what I want, especially with these two wonderful, considerate men.

They spend a few moments sheathing themselves in rubbery protection, and then they're back. Teale's fingers reach between my butt cheeks, coated liberally with what I assume must be lube. It's cold and slippery at first, and then it warms up. He spreads my cheeks and drips more down my seam until my fears about my own wetness fade to nothing. *Jeepers. We'll all slide right off the bed if he's not careful.*

James leans in to kiss me with a warmth that brings tears to my eyes. "Ready?"

I nod and hook one leg over his hips before reaching down to help position him at my entrance. He thrusts a little, breaching my vagina, and then slides in with ease. Just as I imagined, his wide girth is a perfect fit for my greedy channel. The hard, hot flesh fills me to bursting, especially when another push seats him fully inside. He lets out a surprised grunt when I clench my vaginal muscles to hold him tight. *Yes. I've got you, James, and I'm not letting go.* There's something to be said for regular pelvic floor exercises.

Teale's turn now, and I can't help tensing my body again as I feel the tip of his organ pressing against my butthole. "I'll go slow, babe." He kisses the sensitive spot right behind my ear. "Relax. Breathe."

Sure, no problem! I suck in a quick breath and let it out in a hiss when he breaches my body. There's so much lube I can't even say it hurts, beyond a bit of initial stinging. It feels weird though. At first, it's just the tip and he quickly pulls out. Then the next time he pushes in a little further. He repeats the in and out action, slowly, until eventually he's more in than out. I'm so fucking *full* of *man* that there's pressure in every part of my abdomen. I find myself gasping rather than breathing, and I try to slow it down, letting my body get used to their presence. Accepting them in. Welcoming the pressure and enjoying the heaviness and the heat.

When I realize both men are breathing as heavily and

unevenly as me, it sends me right back to the edge of control. They begin to thrust, first James and then Teale, taking it in turns to go in and out, back and forth, with only a thin membrane of flesh within my body separating their plunging organs. They are good at this, obviously practiced, tag-teaming with perfect precision. The realization that my body is cradling two cocks at once and that it feels *fucking fantastic*, pushes my desire to unexpected heights. Sex has never felt like this. The rhythmic movement back and forth, the relentless pounding against my clit and my arse, pleasure and pain deep within my body, the fullness, the unbearable, beautiful *pressure*...

Everything builds until I'm holding onto control by sheer will alone. We rut and fuck and love each other as if there's nothing beyond the here and now. I hear keening, and groans, and animalistic-sounding whimpers, and I don't even know if the noises are coming from me, or James, or Teale. I don't care. All I know is we're balanced together on this crazy precipice, teetering on the edge, and as our love-making escalates I reach a point of no return. "I can't hold on! I'm coming...*coming*... *Oh yes. Fuck* me, both of you!"

We're holding tight to one another's bodies, rocking together as one. James lets out a bellow. "Come baby! I'm coming too. Oh, Teale—"

"*Yes*! *Now*!"

It's not just my clit that blows apart at Teale's hoarse command, it's my vagina, and my arse, and my whole fucking *body* that rockets into the craziest climax of my life. I never knew orgasms like this existed. My scream as the experience rips my body to pieces is closely followed by twin male roars as the three of us fall together into a drowning sea of sensation.

CHAPTER 6

It seems like forever before I come back from wherever I went. Did I black out? I have no idea. Time ceased to exist from the moment I entered that phase of orgasmic pleasure. As I blink and sigh and finally start to become aware of my surroundings once again, I'm grateful to find their arms still wrapped tightly around me. Their touch grounds me. I was everywhere, and nowhere, and now I'm coming back down to a place from which I can begin to process what just happened. *What* did *just happen? It feels like...I died and went to heaven.*

"*Jeez*." James is trembling at least as much as I am, if not more. Teale's arms stretch further and tighten around him as well as me. Our protector.

"You okay, Stace? James? Man, I don't...I can't..." Teale falls silent. It seems even he has no words for what we just experienced.

I bite my lip when I realize my eyes are damp. I've been weeping and didn't even know it, but I don't have enough energy to reach up and wipe away my tears.

James shifts at last, using his thumb to clear the wetness

for me. "Are you okay, Stacey?" He echoes Teale's concern, and I nod weakly.

I'm more than okay, but I'm also shell-shocked. Is this what ménage is like all the time? I suspect not, but it's a relief when Teale presses a kiss to my shoulder and says, "It's never been like that for me before. That was...*amazing*."

"Yeah." James chuckles. "That was the fucking *best* I've ever had."

I let out a giggle, thrilled that this experience was as ground-breaking for them as it was for me. Thrilled that this level of *heaven* wasn't something they've experienced with anyone else. "Don't you mean, the best *fucking* you've ever had?"

Now we all laugh together, perhaps with a common need to release some of the remaining tension. You'd think, after an orgasm that powerful, there'd be no tension left in the room. But, for me at least, there's an element of uncertainty about what comes next.

Laughter's good, but unfortunately the action causes both to slide out of me, first James and then Teale, and I suddenly feel empty as reality rushes back in. When Teale returns from the bathroom, where he's disposed of the condoms and cleaned himself up, he brings a wet wash cloth and towel. He uses it to clean me and dry me off, his strokes as tender as if I'm a baby, and then both men cradle me until eventually, all of us drift off to sleep.

My last thoughts, before I fall into slumber, briefly bring tears once again to my eyes. Because I know deep down that it doesn't matter how good the three of us are together. It doesn't matter if that was the best sex we've ever had. This was simply an impulsive one-night stand, no more nor less than that. We can't keep this up indefinitely unless it always remains a secret from the world, and I know firsthand that secrets destroy lives. I lived with a secret once, and it blew my family apart when the truth accidentally came out. I can't live through anything like that again.

And yet the alternative—being honest about my unconventional desires—would be equally as difficult to live with. I don't think I have the strength to face the resulting gossip and judgement. As wonderful as this night has been with Teale and James, I know that our time together is limited.

This is the first time I've ever woken up in the same bed as two sexy men. I'm sandwiched between them, warm as toast, and their presence makes me feel safe, secure, and far happier than I can remember. Teale is tucked behind me, the big spoon to my smaller one, and James is lying on his stomach, still fast asleep and with one of his arms flung over both my waist and Teale's. His face is turned toward me and in slumber he looks younger than he did last night. More...innocent.

A swell of something far stronger than lust rushes through me, not just for James but also for Teale. The strength of it confuses me. I assumed, when I woke this morning, they'd disappear straight back to their own home across the field, and that would be the end of it. I figured I'd then spend an inordinate amount of time trying to get over my guilt at participating in something so dirty.

But what we did doesn't feel dirty. Instead it's as if the three of us are meant to be together. A big part of me doesn't understand why it seems so right. The experience is so foreign to anything I've ever done, and I'm already worrying about what people might think if they ever find out about our ménage secret.

I tuck those misgivings into the back of my mind when Teale's erection stirs against my butt and I see the flutter of James's eyelids as he begins to wake. These men made me feel cherished last night, something I haven't experienced in a long time. Surely here, in the privacy of my home and the cocoon of my bed, it's safe to forget about everyone else? At least for one more day.

James rolls onto his side and stretches. His eyes open fully and he breaks into a radiant smile when he sees me. It's one of those smiles that causes the recipient's heart to fill with joy. "Hello, gorgeous." His morning voice is just as gruff as usual, but his touch, when he reaches up to shift a lock of hair out of my eyes, is gentle.

"Good morning." I cup his cheek in return, and he leans in to give me a kiss. The action doesn't have the urgency associated with last night's coupling. Instead, there's a tenderness in our connection that's stronger than before. Behind me Teale also shifts. One of his hands begins to trace random patterns over my waist and hip. His erection is no longer stirring but demanding attention. I roll onto my back and allow him to kiss me too. "Good morning to both of you. Looks like last night wasn't enough for...*oh*! For *either* one of you."

James is tenting the bed as effectively as Teale, and I now have two morning erections willing and ready. I reach down under the covers to find and caress their ridged lengths, marveling once again at the differences between them, even though the heat and the hardness are essentially the same. I work a little faster, enjoying the shudder from Teale and the faint groan from James. Their dual manhood is literally in the palm of my hands. I love having this much power, and I move faster still, filled with the need to give them as much pleasure as they provided me last night.

Teale is clearly further along than James and his breathing

is short and harsh. I pause, helping James to catch up, and then they're both groaning and shuddering and almost ready to come. I kick the bed covers out of the way and wriggle down until their cocks are right in front of my face.

James briefly raises his head from the pillow and stares down at me. "If you use your mouth I'll be done in seconds."

"Good." I tease the tip of him with my thumb and feel the answering spurt of pre-cum, slick and wet. "How about you, Teale?" I do the same to his member and his grunt sounds almost like he's in pain.

"Fuck yes. I'm *there*. It... I'm ready to *explode*, Stace."

"Even better." I urge them together until their tips are slip-sliding against one another and I have what looks like one enormous cock sausage laid out in front of me. The urge to laugh almost overcomes me, but I swallow it down. I have no idea what I'm doing. Not with two of them. *Guess I'll have to wing it.*

I position myself more comfortably, lying across their tangled legs, and run my mouth along the full length of their dicks, nibbling from the base of Teale all the way through to the base of James and back again. I cup their balls in my hands and tease gently, first one and then the other, pressing into the sensitive spot behind their sacs and enjoying the heartfelt groans that fill the room. Then I separate them and get to work. The sticky pre-cum makes it super-easy to slide first one and then the other into my mouth and throat. I work fast, swapping from one to the other and using my lips, tongue, and teeth to elicit a response. Whatever I'm doing seems to be working, because both of them are moaning and I can feel the trembling of multiple legs pinned beneath my body.

I take advantage of one of those legs—I think maybe it's Teale—and rub my hungry clit against his hard flesh as I continue to suck and blow on their organs. The wiry hair on his leg adds to the friction and the pleasure in my cunt rises in unison with their desire. Their unique flavors have combined to create the most delicious tang and I just can't get enough. I pull one of them so far in the head of his cock hits the back of my throat and I almost gag. Then he's out and the other replaces him. And so it goes on, back and forth. In and out. Until the drawing up of their balls beneath my questing hands signals a sudden increase in tension and at the exact same moment they both let out a guttural cry and release their load. Cum explodes everywhere in a fountain of creamy seed, shooting up into the air before raining down over all three of us. The sensory overload is too much and I let go too, bucking crazily on Teale's willing leg in an orgasm so strong it almost splits me in two. Afterwards I lay tangled amongst their legs, slick with cum and panting hard. I have no energy, not enough even to crawl back up the bed to somewhere slightly more comfortable. Eventually Teale lifts me, gently. Each man throws an arm across my middle.

After several minutes, I attempt to speak. "Wow." Nothing else seems appropriate.

James snickers, and Teale's crooked grin appears. "Yeah. Wow, indeed." He shifts onto one elbow and stares down at me. "I'm so glad we were late back from our night out and had the chance to meet you at last, Stacey. I mean, not good that you broke down, of course, but we can sort that out for you."

"It'd be awesome if you could help get me back on the road. And, maybe I can cook you both a dinner soon to say thanks?"

Where did that come from? Wasn't this supposed to be a one night only thing? But they're both nodding, and I can't take back the words that make this something potentially...*more.* "That'd be great, Stace." James casts a glance toward his friend. "Teale's a shitty cook to be honest, so if I want something good to eat I usually have to cook it myself. It'll be nice to have someone else do that for once."

Teale shrugs. "I wish I could say he's joking, but he's kinda not. Even *I* wouldn't eat what I make. I've got a better idea though. Why don't we all go out for dinner? We can show you our favorite place for—"

"No." I quickly shake my head, and Teale's brows come together in a confused frown. I try to explain. "No, I can't... not out in public..."

Confusion clears from his gaze and dismay takes its place. "Ah. So it's like that, then."

James shifts beside me. "Like what? *Oh.*" He too has just realized what I knew all along. That this thing between us has no future outside these four walls.

I'm not sure what changes, but there's a sudden chill in the air that wasn't evident a few seconds earlier. I've offended them, and I don't need extra-sensory perception to figure that out. They stare at me in accusatory silence.

"I'm sorry." It seems inadequate, after the night we've just shared, and my heart aches at the thought of letting them disappear from my life. But I've only just moved here to try and put the past behind me, and we all know it isn't morally acceptable to be in a relationship with more than one person at a time, at least not in our society. I owe them both an explanation.

"Okay. So." This is harder than I expect and I have to take a deep breath to steady myself before continuing. "I was the laughing stock of our whole community when my husband left." It's *much* harder than I expect. "All the school crowd, the soccer moms, even some members of my own family. They stopped talking to me when they found out I already knew about my husband *shtooping* the housekeeper." Teale's mouth drops open and I wave a hand to keep him quiet while I try to explain the unexplainable.

"It's like I was paralyzed when I found out it had been going on for several months. I couldn't react; couldn't do anything. Now that I've had some counselling I get that I was most likely in shock or denial, but at the time it probably seemed like I didn't care. So he flaunted it, and I shut down even more, and when everyone inevitably found out, my inaction somehow became an even bigger betrayal than my ex's infidelity. Fair or not, that's how our kids saw it, too—that's how *everyone* saw it—and I ended up becoming the woman who let her husband and her *children* run off with the housekeeper. I'm the woman who lost her *whole family* to the other woman because I didn't speak up about what was morally right or wrong."

CHAPTER 7

There. It's out, at last. The sordid truth of my past. James huffs a breath and looks away, then back again, as if taking a moment to process what I've said. Teale's gaze reflects shock. "Fuck," he says. "That's rough."

I let out a laugh, but it sounds more brittle than I intend. "Yeah. It *was* pretty rough for a while. The pitying looks, the judgmental stares. The speculation about why even my *kids* ran away from me. From one day to the next, all the people I thought were friends suddenly stopped calling or talking to me. Maybe they didn't want to be tainted."

Tears threaten and I swallow down the hard lump in my throat. This is the first time I've spoken with anyone outside immediate family—and my counsellor—about what happened, and it brings back more bad feelings than I expect. Hell, it's been over two years. You'd think the pain would be minimal by now.

Teale cups the back of my neck, massaging gently. James strokes my thigh. These men are so genuinely caring, and yet they hardly know me. Their kindness acts like a catalyst for

JEN KATEMI

my threatened tears which brim over, wetting my cheeks. The pain clenching at my throat is so deeply embedded it feels like earache.

"I was the perfect wife. The perfect mother. Or so I thought." This confession is fucking *hard*, but I've spent so long analyzing *why*, and I owe Teale and James the truth. At least, the truth as I understand it with the added benefit of hindsight. "I wasn't, though. Perfect, that is. I was so caught up in trying to be flawless, and to behave in the way that I thought everyone expected, that I switched off to what was *real*. My husband had needs that I didn't even *see*, and my children...my own *children*..."

A sob escapes, despite my efforts to hold it in. Both of Teale's hands knead my shoulders and there's a gentleness in his touch and in the rhythm of his movement that soothes my jangled emotions. I lean back against his firm chest, taking strength from the connection. Beside me, James continues to stroke my naked thigh, and I reach down to capture his wandering hand. Our fingers link, holding tight. I take a deep breath and blurt out the worst bit. "My children needed *me*, and I gave them a robot on auto-pilot. I don't blame them for choosing to live primarily with their dad. Especially when he can offer a rather awesome place right on the beach that's perfect for teenage boys who love to surf."

Both my sons have been back several times to Melbourne and we've worked through a lot of the angst of those early days. I've been over to Perth twice now to visit them in their new location. It was difficult at first, but they're thriving at their new school and while the cross-country separation isn't what I want, it's what they seem to need, at least for now.

I'm lost in my own thoughts until James squeezes my hand, re-focusing my attention. "So, I guess you don't have to worry about the cleanliness of their new house," he says.

"Seeing as how your ex chose a housekeeper to run off with 'n all."

"*James*!" Teale stiffens instantly and I can tell he's concerned about my reaction, but when our cheeky companion slants a look my way and wiggles his eyebrows up and down, my tears suddenly give way to hilarity. Somewhat hysterical hilarity, perhaps, but it beats crying. The hurt recedes, and eventually I nod.

"I'm sure she does a much better job than I could, in that respect at least."

Teale relaxes behind me, and I turn my head and rub my cheek against his chest to reassure him. "I'm fine, really. But you see, I can't…I just can't…face the thought of public scrutiny and speculation all over again."

James reclines against one of the pillows and tucks his hands behind his head. "Fuck what everyone else thinks, Stace. *We* don't care. We never have. Rules are made to be broken. That's our philosophy of life and to be perfectly honest, everyone already knows how we live and no one here seems to care."

Teale is quieter in his response. "We disagree with your reasoning, love. But we won't push, if you don't want to be seen out in public with us like that. I get it. *We* get it. Don't we, James?"

"Yeah." James picks at the edge of the bedcover. "Don't like it, mind you."

I know I've let them down, but I can't change how I feel. Outside these four walls, I'm desperate to be seen as Miss Average. I can't bear the thought of gossip or innuendo, and I don't want to be known as the woman who rolled into town and immediately started indulging in a threesome with the sexy mechanics next door.

"I'm sorry." I say it again, and this time there's a sense of finality. All I want to do is burst into tears when first James, and then Teale, slides out of the bed.

"So are we, honey. More sorry than you'll ever know." Regret laces Teale's words. Somehow, I manage to hold in the tears until both men are dressed and gone. When the front door snicks shut behind them, I realize I've never felt more alone in my life.

Teale

Things aren't right in our lives. Things haven't been right since the morning we left Stacey's bed. It's like we lost an important piece of ourselves that day. I can't stop sniping at James, and vice versa, over even the smallest of things.

She's avoided us since then, even when we fixed her car and James drove it back over to her cute little cottage. He knocked but she didn't answer, so we left the car key in the letterbox with a note. A couple of days later we got a polite thank you note in return, together with some money to cover the repairs and our time. *What is she thinking? That we won't be able to keep our hands to ourselves if we lay eyes on her again?*

I'm fuming, and James is sulking. We're both walking around with permanent semi-hard-ons, to the point where James slides into my bed one night and we suck each other off. We've done that before, in dry spells between women, but this time it's different. This time it feels wrong, as if we're cheating on our partner, and even though James is damn good with his mouth, my orgasm is muted and uneventful. A pure physical release without the enhancement of any emotional connection beyond friendship.

Pretty sure James feels the same way. His hot seed spills into my mouth and down my chin with only a tiny grunt from him to convey the impact, and then he's gone, sliding out from under the covers and back to his own bedroom without any words being spoken. He looks hollow-eyed, poor guy. I think he's getting as little sleep as I am right now.

I almost punch him in the face when I find out he's ordered some of her soap online. She probably got a bit of a shock when she received *that* order, but instead of hand-delivering it herself the way he's clearly expecting, the package arrives in the post. Just like any other regular anonymous order.

Fuck's sake. She must have taken it to the local post office for mailing. Bet *they* had a damn good laugh before they dropped it back in our local box.

Now we both smell like Stacey, all fresh lemon and eucalyptus, and it's driving me even more insane. We're taking showers at all times of the day and night, lathering up with her goddamn soap so we can get a visceral whiff of the woman in the only way we can. Via her delicious scented product that evokes tantalizing memories of our entwined rutting bodies every time I move.

To be honest I can't concentrate on anything except our neighbor's cottage on the hill. I stare toward it every time I walk between our house and the garage, wondering if she's observing us from one of those darkened windows. Wondering if she misses us. Wondering why it's so difficult for some people to throw off the shackles of conformity and just live their lives the way they want, without regard for what others think.

"You know she's watching, don't you? I feel it." James hands me a beer and joins me on the old settee on our porch.

It's sunset, and I'm sitting here staring out toward Stacey's house.

"Yeah. I feel it too."

"It's driving me insane." His admission shocks me. James is always so guarded with his emotions.

"Me too." I take a sip of beer.

"It was one night of damn good sex. Why can't we just put it behind us and move on, like we usually do?"

There's no answer I can give that makes sense, so I just shrug and drink more beer. A simple one-night stand shouldn't have this much impact on our mood.

"What are we gonna do, Teale? Can't we just, I don't know, continue to see her in secret? We can sneak over there after dark and be back home before morning. No one else ever needs to know."

I'm tempted, but in the end I shake my head. "That might work for us, for a while, but I have the feeling it wouldn't suit Stace. And besides, this feels different, James, at least to me. This feels like it has the potential to develop into...*something*."

He nods quietly. I'm not telling him anything he doesn't already know. I surprise myself as much as James when I burst out, "I'm *mad* at her for not at least giving us a chance beyond that one night."

He briefly touches my thigh. "I get it, T. I feel the same way. But at least we've still got each other."

"True." We've always had each other, and I know that will never change. I love James, and I know he loves me in return. It was just that this time, with Stacey, I thought maybe we might have the opportunity for something more. *I hoped for so much.* We sit in silence, sipping our beers and watching the sun go down. "It has to be her decision," I continue at last. "If there's any chance at all that she might want to see us again, she'll have to come to us."

James shrugs, his eyes reflecting uncertainty.

We need patience. It was such a brief encounter, but the effect of her presence—and now her absence—is ongoing, and it hurts.

CHAPTER 8

STACEY

I can't believe it's been two weeks since that night. Meeting Teale and James changed *everything*. It's as if that night presented me with a crossroads decision for the future, and somehow I managed to choose the wrong path. Since then it feels as if I've been marching in the opposite direction to where I should be headed, but turning around would mean committing to something I'm not sure I'm ready for.

How can one night of sex have such a lasting impact? It's *crazy*. I hardly know them, and they certainly don't know much about me beyond what I'm like in bed.

I left the city to escape the judgmental looks and censure from everyone I know except my two sisters. *Everyone*. Without my sisters I might not be alive today. I didn't let on to Teale and James, but my depression became so severe after the boys left that I ended up in hospital. It's been a long hard journey since then to try and re-establish my place and my purpose in life. I set up here in Peaceton precisely because it is somewhere completely different from everything I've known in the past. I wanted to start fresh, among people who don't know me at all. People who aren't going to judge me.

Logically, I know that one of the reasons my ex and my kids now live on the other side of the country is because I strove for perfection above all else. Because I chose image over reality. Because I cared, too much, about what the outside world thinks, to the detriment of my family's needs.

And now, I'm doing it again. Pushing Teale and James away because I'm scared about what people might think. I sit here in this rural location, living alone and working an online business that allows me to be part of society without direct face-to-face connection. Because it's so much easier to liaise remotely than try to deal with real flesh-and-blood people. It's the perfect life for a recluse, and until I met Teale and James, it *was* the perfect new life for me.

But it isn't, anymore. From the moment I met my sexy neighbors I began to fall for them both, and in that unexpected development I became someone more than a recluse. I became someone who has been given a rare second chance at life. Someone for whom the possibility of a loving relationship is suddenly no longer a pipe dream. But in order to explore that faint possibility for happiness, I'm going to have to face everything I'm afraid of. Do I have the courage to carry through with it? Do I have the inner strength to drop my guard and let them in? I don't know. I simply don't know.

James

"Delicious as always, Jamie. We're lucky to have your cooking skills for the fair every year."

I hand out another plate to those crowding our stall, and smile at the elderly woman who has just taken a second bite of my carrot cake. "Couldn't leave it to Teale, now, could I, Rosie? You'd never raise any funds off of *his* cooking."

A burst of laughter breaks out around us and I slant a look toward Teale. He rolls his eyes dramatically before continuing to cut and plate up cake as fast as he can. We do this every year at the local community fair, and our stall is always popular. I like to think it's my cooking skills that attract everyone, but Teale always says it's 'cos everyone is fascinated by the idea that two muscled mechanics can actually bake cakes and muffins. Well, *one* of us can, at least. Teale's strength lies in serving them up. And eating.

He starts to hand me another plate, but it drops out of his grip and falls to the ground before I can save it. I open my mouth to ask *what the hell*, but he's staring over my shoulder as if he's seen a ghost. From his reaction, I know instantly who'll be standing there when I turn, but it's still a shock when I see Stacey in the midst of the crowd around our stall. My heart kicks right up into my mouth and straight back down again. *Holy crap.* All I can think, when I see her trying to worm her way through to the front, is how good it felt to bed myself deep inside her accommodating body. I loved being inside her. It felt so fucking right. My cock twitches in an ill-timed reminder and I shift uncomfortably, trying to tamp my physical response back down.

She's so tiny it takes a bit of time to force her way through the crowd. Enough time that I can remind my lungs it's okay to start working once again. "Um…" I swallow, unable to say anything, tongue-tied and praying for some kind of deliverance from this acute anxiety that flares the moment she reaches our stall table.

Teale, as always, is ahead of me in that respect. He stops cutting cake and steps forward to position himself by my side. We stand arm to arm, a solid unit facing our nemesis across the stack of cakes. The woman with the potential to wound our pride, and perhaps our hearts.

Stacey. Please don't reject us again.

She stares from me to Teale and back again, her mouth working convulsively, and though I can appreciate how nervous she must be, I heed Teale's silent message to wait. He's right. Anything that transpires from this moment forward has to come first from her, and we need to be patient so that our response will be the right one. For all of us.

"I was wrong," she says, and then swallows hard. "Can I..." She glances at the people around us and then back to Teale. "Do you mind if I announce it?"

It? What does she mean? I turn my head just in time to catch the flare of joy that radiates from Teale's fixed gaze. *He* gets it, whatever *it* is. He starts nodding, and his fingers interlace with mine behind our cake mix-crusted aprons. "We've never hidden who or what our relationship is, Stace. Everyone here knows, and we're comfortable with whatever it is you'd like to say."

Oh! That "it." *Is she really...* My heart starts pounding even harder, and sudden excitement rushes through my veins. I gesture for her to come around the table. When she's finally standing between us, Teale and I each put an arm around her. As if they can sense something important, the crowd nearby falls silent. They're ogling the three of us, curious at what's about to happen.

Stacey clears her throat. "I have an announcement." There's an edge of tension in her tone and I give her a squeeze of encouragement.

Go girl. You can do this.

"A *community* announcement, I guess, seeing as how this is a community fair."

Teale adjusts his grip. We're both holding on so tight

she's never going to escape us now. *We're here for you. You're not alone.*

"So. Yeah. My name is Stacey Gamble, and I think a lot of you know me as the 'soap woman'." She pauses to look down at the ground, and then lifts her chin, facing them all. "I want to thank you for welcoming me in to your community these past few months. Peaceton is a lovely place to live. I also want to let you know that Teale and James and I, well, we're…" She stops, and then blurts out in a rush. "We're kind of…seeing each other. Well, I hope we are, anyway." Her face turns bright red as she speaks, but she's still holding her chin high. I want to laugh at her awkward wording, but I'm so fucking *proud* of her in this moment that the urge to laugh fades to nothing. Her rapid breathing flutters against me.

"We are," Teale confirms in a loud tone.

I nod too, before leaning in to whisper in Stacey's ear, "We've got you, babe."

She flicks me a quick glance. "I know," she says, and I feel her arm creep around my waist. It feels *right*. She faces the crowd again. "I want to be with them…if they'll have me…but I won't do it in secret. Even if it breaks all the rules of what people think is right. So…" She takes a deep breath and lets it out slowly, then turns in our arms so that she's speaking directly to us and no one else. "I'm falling for you both, Teale and James. I can't choose between you, and in truth I don't want to. I'd like to see where this goes, all three of us together, and I hope you feel the same—"

She doesn't finish. She can't. Teale and I embrace her so tightly there's no room left for words. I press a light kiss on the top of her head, as does Teale. We deliberately keep it chaste in deference to the crowd, but there's a spark that flares between us at the moment of connection. *Oh boy. This could be the real deal.*

I'm vaguely aware of cheering, and when we turn back to the crowd there's a sea of smiling faces and clapping hands. I squeeze Stacey and she lets out a tiny squeak. "See?" I tease. "Not as hard as you thought, was it?"

She elbows me in the ribs. "It was much harder than I thought, you bloody annoying man. They'll probably be talking about us for the next ten years. But I'm so relieved. No more secrets."

"And...*happy*?" Teale's tentative query floats quietly through the air and she nods vigorously. I'm nodding too, positive this big grin splitting my face looks stupid. I can't help it. I can't contain my happiness.

"Oh yes!" Her smile breaks free at last and it's radiant. "So very happy. It's different this time. I'm not alone. I have you both by my side, and to be honest there's no place in the world I'd rather be than right here, right now, with the two of you. I can't wait to spend more time with you. Learn more about each other, and...see where this goes from here."

"Sounds like a plan," Teale says.

"Sounds like a damn *good* plan." When I echo Teale's words, Stacey punches me gently in the arm.

He hands me a plate of cake, and then passes one over to Stace, and together, the three of us turn back to the crowd to continue our task of raising funds for the community. *Together*. I like the sound of that. Big time.

The End

ABOUT THE AUTHOR

Jen Katemi is an award-winning and bestselling author of steamy contemporary romance. She is published with Evernight Publishing, Naughty Nights Press, and as Jennifer Lynne with Red Sage. She has also forged a successful indie career starting with her popular GODS OF LOVE and FORBIDDEN series of erotic novellas.

When she's not writing, Jen works in admin, looks after the family, pampers various cats, and tries to find a smidgen of time for her husband. She lives in Melbourne, Australia.

Find out more at Jen's website:
www.JenKatemi.com